WYOMING'S MOST ELIGIBLE BACHELORS

1. Chad Randall
2. Pete Randall
3. Brett Randall
4. Jake Randall

Cons	Pros
hard-hearted	good-lookin'
mule-headed	hot-blooded
love 'em & leave 'em	rough & ready

No contest—the Randall brothers are the best catch in the county!

Their response: "Wild horses can't make us take a wife!"

Dear Reader,

I'm so excited to introduce you to Jake Randall and his three brothers—Chad, Pete and Brett. You'll be reading all about them in my new miniseries, 4 BRIDES FOR 4 BROTHERS, starting this month.

I love big families who care about each other, and I love cowboys! Out there on their Wyoming ranch, the Randall brothers fill both bills. As oldest brother and keeper of the family, Jake feels responsible for the fact that none of his brothers has married, so he sets out to play cupid for them. Like most big brothers, he thinks he knows best. And like most younger siblings, Chad, Pete and Brett don't cooperate! Their stories will make you laugh and make you want to join the Randalls in their pursuit of love.

I hope you'll join me and the Randall brothers for all four books in the 4 BRIDES FOR 4 BROTHERS series!

Happy reading!

Judy Christenberry

Judy Christenberry

COWBOY CUPID

Harlequin Books

TORONTO • NEW YORK • LONDON
AMSTERDAM • PARIS • SYDNEY • HAMBURG
STOCKHOLM • ATHENS • TOKYO • MILAN
MADRID • WARSAW • BUDAPEST • AUCKLAND

ISBN 0-373-16649-4

COWBOY CUPID

Chapter One

Chad Randall took another sip of coffee, watching his brother Jake pace the kitchen floor.

"What's up, Jake?" he finally asked.

His brother's head jerked around as if Chad had roped him. "What?"

"What's got you so stirred up? You've been walking the floor the last ten minutes. Has the bottom fallen out of the beef market?"

"No. Where are your brothers?"

"They went to the barn. Said they'd be back in a little while." It wasn't like Jake to be so antsy.

Jake checked his watch and walked to the window over the sink.

"It's Sunday afternoon, Jake. Our one time to relax. Even if there's snow on the ground, the sun's shining. Everything's doing fine." When his brother didn't answer, Chad prodded, "Right?"

"Uh, yeah, right."

"Good thing you're not trying to sell me anything," Chad drawled.

Again Jake whirled around. "What do you mean?"

"You're not very convincing. Come clean."

Jake stared at Chad, reminding him of times in the past when he'd incurred Jake's censure. He frantically searched his memory to see if he was in trouble, but he could remember nothing that would upset Jake. At least not much.

"Okay, here's the deal," Jake said at last with a rush of breath. "We're going to have company."

"So?"

"Female company."

Jake's blunt words stunned Chad. "Female company?" he echoed. "You been seeing someone, Jake?"

"No!" he roared. "No, of course not, you idiot!"

"Well, hell, Jake, what was I to think? What female company are you talking about?" The Randalls weren't women haters, by any means. In fact, Chad, the youngest of the Randall boys, loved women—*all* women. But after Jake's divorce, none of them had gotten serious about women.

"Do you remember me going to Denver?"

"'Course I do. That conference in pasture management."

"Well, I also hired some decorators."

Chad looked around him. He didn't see anything wrong with their home. "Why?"

"The place needs fixing up."

"Okay. But why from Denver?" There was something going on here, Chad was sure, but he couldn't figure out what.

"Why not? We want the best."

"Hell, Jake, it'll cost you twice as much as a decorator from Casper or Cheyenne. This lady might even expect to stay overnight."

"*These* ladies," Jake muttered.

Chad slapped his cup down on the table. "Two? You've got two ladies coming?"

"Three."

His eyes widening in surprise, Chad leaned back against the chair and stared at his brother. "Three?" he repeated faintly.

"Yeah. We had to have a choice." Jake paused, frowning. Before Chad could question his strange statement, he added, "A choice of decor, I mean. Each decorator will draw up some plans, and we'll choose the one we like best."

"Okay. Have you told Red?" The old cowboy who took care of them would be the one most affected by the changes.

"Just that we were having visitors."

"So what's the plan? We show them around this afternoon, then they go back to Denver and draw up their plans?"

"Uh, not exactly."

Again that feeling that something was going on that he didn't yet understand filled Chad. "What do you mean?"

"They'll have to stay a little longer."

"Tomorrow? They'll go back tomorrow."

Jake shook his head.

"How long are we going to have to have these women here, Jake? And what in hell are we going to do with them? We're not used to having women around."

"A week. They have to stay a week."

"A week? Three women here for a week?" Chad demanded, rising to his feet. "We can't—" He broke off as a thought occurred to him. "What do they look like? You got designs on any of these women?"

He did a double take when Jake didn't offer him an immediate no. He'd been teasing, sure Jake would reject such an idea. The fact that he didn't left Chad uneasy. Was Jake back in the marriage market?

MEGAN CHASE'S GAZE MET the lady's next to her.

"Bit remote, isn't it?" Adele Paxton observed, one eyebrow rising.

She nodded. "Were you given much information about the job?"

Adele started to answer, but the young woman sitting across from them in the limo interrupted. "It's a complete redo for a wealthy rancher. We're competing against each other, you know." Her self-satisfied smirk made Megan think Rita Larson was confident she would win.

"Yes, I know, but did you get any more details?" she asked.

"No, but even if I had, I wouldn't tell you," Rita replied. "After all, why help my competition?"

"I wasn't told any more," Adele added. Her gray hair was cut short and stylishly coiffed. "Though I understand Mr. Randall requested we all be single. My boss thought it was strange, but Mr. Randall explained that he didn't want any jealous husbands upset because everyone on the ranch is a man.''

Megan had also thought that request was a little bizarre, but her employer had assured her everything was on the up-and-up. She'd been with the interior-design firm since her graduation a little over three years ago, but this was her first solo project.

"You must have a lot of experience," she murmured to Adele. The woman appeared to be around fifty, though she'd aged well.

"Yes, I suppose so."

"It's the creative spark that's important, not experience," Rita snapped, frowning at both of them. Then she looked directly at Megan. "Of course, you, poor dear, probably don't have either."

Megan raised her eyebrows and smiled slightly. If Rita Larson thought she could intimidate her competition, she had another thought coming. "Really? You've seen my work, Rita? I've seen yours."

Though she had carefully said nothing offensive, Megan wasn't surprised when Rita got upset. Sputtering, she tried to protest.

"Look," Adele said in a warning voice, "if we're going to be here a week, we'd best put aside any petty behavior and cooperate."

Megan appreciated Adele's words. She had let her temper get the better of her. Still, she had no intention of allowing Rita Larson—or anyone—to verbally assault her. Megan was nothing if not assertive. Over the years, she'd learned to look out for herself. She had to: her mother had married five times. Good for Lila, as each husband got progressively wealthier.

While Megan had enjoyed helping her mother with the redecorating—with each marriage, a total redo was imperative, according to Lila—she'd hated dealing with the heartache of each divorce. She learned the only reliable person in her life was herself—and she'd promised herself she'd never marry and allow anyone to do such damage to her heart.

"How much farther?" Rita demanded of the driver.

"According to the map, the turnoff should be soon." He kept his eyes on the road, scarcely paying them any attention.

That behavior suited Megan, but Rita seemed peeved by it. "Can't you tell us something about the area?" she asked.

"No, ma'am. I just moved to Casper last month."

"It doesn't matter," she snapped back. "I've done my research." She turned a triumphant look on the others, as if it wouldn't have occurred to them to check out some facts about Wyoming.

Megan tried to hide her grin. She wasn't going to purposefully irritate Rita Larson if she could help it, but the woman certainly did offer herself as a prime target.

The limo slowed down and turned off the main road. All three women leaned forward to catch the first sight of the ranch house they were going to be working on.

All they saw was pastureland with mountains in the background.

"Where's the house?" Rita demanded of the driver.

"I don't know, ma'am. We'll just follow this road and see if we find it."

Megan exchanged a smile with Adele. The driver's words were polite, but there was a note of impatience in them.

"I hope we get to ride horses. I've never been on a ranch," Rita told them.

Adele only raised an eyebrow in response, and Megan said nothing. Her mother's second husband had had a ranch in Colorado. That's why Megan had chosen Denver after college. She'd fallen in love with the area.

She wouldn't mind doing some riding while she was here, but she doubted there would be time. Redoing an entire house would take a lot of planning.

"There's the house," Adele said quietly.

"It's large," Megan murmured, training her eyes on the small speck on the horizon.

"Look, there are some other buildings, too." Rita pointed, bringing another grin to Megan's face.

"There usually are on a ranch. Bunkhouse, barns, storage sheds."

"How do you know so much about it?" Rita demanded, frowning at Megan.

Unable to resist, Megan smiled and said, "Research."

WHEN CHAD HEARD FOOTSTEPS on the back porch, he straightened in his chair. He couldn't wait to see how Jake informed his brothers of their guests' arrival.

"Hey, Jake," Brett said as they entered the kitchen. "Did you put the bill for the feed on my desk? I didn't find it, and the delivery is here."

"Bill hasn't come yet."

Pete ignored everyone and headed for the coffeepot. Since he'd broken up with Janie, a neighbor, he seldom spoke to anyone. Chad knew his brothers, as well as himself, were worried about Pete, but the second brother shrugged off any attempt to cheer him up.

Maybe that's why Jake had decided to have the house redone, Chad thought. To take Pete's mind off Janie. Chad didn't think silk pillows and fancy lamps would do it, but you never knew.

"What are you grinning about?" Pete growled as he sat down beside him.

"Uh, nothing. 'Cept maybe your reaction to Jake's news." A quick look at Jake had Chad wishing he'd kept his mouth shut.

"What news?" Pete demanded, looking at Jake.

Jake gave a succinct account of his plan.

Red entered the kitchen, vacuum cleaner in hand, just in time to hear the news. "Hey, Jake, does that mean the kitchen will be redone?"

Jake pulled his gaze from his brothers'. "I guess, Red, if there's anything you want changed."

"Hellfire, boy! Of course there's things I want done. Some modern equipment wouldn't hurt. A new floor that's easy to clean. An up-to-date dishwasher would be a miracle."

The brothers all stared at the man who had essentially been their mother since Chad was born.

"Why didn't you say anything before?" Brett asked.

"I didn't want to cause no trouble. And I don't know what I want 'cause I'm never in a store. 'Ceptin' the grocery store to buy more supplies for you human vacuum cleaners."

Jake patted him on the shoulder. "You can have whatever you want, Red. You deserve it. When the ladies get here, we'll tell 'em to work with you." After Red happily left to put away his cleaning equipment, Jake turned back to his brothers.

"I expect you all to be on your best behavior. And Pete, since you're second-in-command, I thought maybe you'd show the ladies around. Explain the setup."

"Brett or Chad can do that," Pete growled, not looking up from his coffee.

"I think you'd be the better man for the job," Jake insisted. "Those two can't be trusted around a bunch of pretty women."

Pete frowned even more. "I'm not interested in any ladies."

"Exactly. So you'll be the perfect host," Jake agreed, a gleam in his eye that reminded Chad of his earlier suspicions.

"Don't worry, brother," Brett said, slapping Pete on the shoulder. "If they're good-looking, you won't be alone."

Jake stepped closer to the table. "You and Chad are to take care of business and leave the women to Pete."

Brett started to protest, but Chad interrupted him. "They're probably all married, Brett."

"Nope." Jake's unequivocal response had everyone staring at him.

"How do you know?" Chad asked.

"Because I made that a requirement," Jake said. "Since we're all men here, I didn't want any complaints from a lot of husbands."

Chad looked at his three brothers. He could understand what Jake was saying. They were an impressive quartet, even if he had to say so himself.

Even more than his good looks, Jake had a reputation for honesty and strength throughout the state. Chloe may have considered him poor husband material, complaining that he worked too much and led a boring life, but Chad figured if Jake so much as hinted that he wanted to remarry, there'd be a line forming all the way to the state border.

"I hear a car," Jake suddenly said. "Come on. I want all of you out front to greet our guests."

Force of habit had his brothers following Jake. Chad was certainly curious to see the women who would invade the all-male environment on the Randall ranch.

And he couldn't wait to see which woman was going to be the first in line to try to rope and hog-tie Jake.

Was their male bastion about to change again? Chad only hoped Jake made a better choice this time.

The limo came to a stop, and Jake moved down the steps to open the door to the long vehicle, eager expectation filling his face. He looked like a lottery player, his ticket clutched in his hand, waiting for the right numbers to be called.

One long, silk-stockinged leg came through the open door, and Chad took a deep breath. Maybe Jake had hit pay dirt after all.

Chapter Two

Megan was the first out of the limo. She didn't see the reception committee until she'd moved aside for the other two women to emerge. Then her gaze collided with four pairs of brown eyes.

"Oh, my," she murmured, stunned by the sight of four large, handsome men, casually dressed in tight jeans, boots and flannel shirts, staring at her. They were an impressive array of testosterone.

"Well, well, well," Rita crooned as she joined Megan. "I think I *love* Wyoming."

"Glad to hear it," one of the cowboys said, moving forward. "I'm Jake Randall. Welcome." He extended a large hand first to Rita and then Megan.

When Adele emerged from the limo, Megan noticed a frown appear on the man's handsome features. But it quickly disappeared as he welcomed the older woman, too.

"Let me introduce my brothers." Each of the men tipped his hat to the ladies as Jake presented him, much like the cowboys in movies, Megan thought with a smile. In fact, any of the four men would make a good living in Hollywood, she surmised, whether they could act or not. Women would pay money just to look at them.

"Come on in out of the cold," Jake invited.

Megan noted that the four men wore no coats, while she and the other two city ladies were bundled in overcoats. It was a sunshiny January day, but the high hovered somewhere around freezing.

The limo driver was unloading their bags, and two of the Randall brothers stayed behind to collect them. Jake and the fourth brother escorted them into the house.

When one of them touched Megan on the shoulder, she turned to discover him smiling, his brown eyes warm as he said, "Hey, pretty lady, can I take your coat?"

"Yes, thank you." In spite of the way her heart leapt at his sexy tones, she kept her voice as cool and crisp as the mountain air. Just because a good-looking cowboy paid her some attention, she wasn't about to lose her head. A flirtation wasn't on her list of things to do.

Rita, on the other hand, cozied up to the man, leaning toward him. "Which one are you? You're all so gorgeous I forgot to pay attention to the names."

"I'm Chad, ma'am," he said with a grin, helping her out of her coat. "And I think the word *gorgeous* might be better used for you ladies. We haven't had such attractive visitors in a long time." His gaze slid to Megan's, as if checking her reaction to his flattery, but she turned away.

Megan discovered Adele staring at their surroundings, and she was reminded of their reason for being there. It didn't take long to realize their work was cut out for them. The entry hall was wide, well proportioned, but it had a neglected air to it. The delicate table along one wall seemed out of place, uncared for.

Jake gestured for them to come into the first room on the right, and Megan couldn't hold back a gasp when she entered. The huge room, clearly the living room, had picture-frame windows along the front of the house. The other end was dominated by a huge stone fireplace. In between were odds and ends of furniture worn out by, she suspected, the size of the four men.

A decorator's dream.

She and Adele exchanged excited smiles.

"We thought you might like a cup of coffee to warm you up before going to your rooms," Jake explained as he invited them to sit down.

An older man, with the stamp of cowboy on him in spite of his gray hair, entered the room carrying a large tray. He was followed by the other two brothers.

"I'd like you to meet Red. He takes care of us," Jake said, looping an arm across the smaller man's shoulders. "And he wants you to fix up the kitchen, as well as the rest of the house."

Adele and Megan nodded, smiling at Red. Rita, who was momentarily distracted from Chad, said, "Oh, I know the perfect thing. Tile imported from Italy with hand-painted flowers on them. It's the latest rage. You'll adore it!''

Megan and Adele looked at each other but remained silent. Rita hadn't done enough research if she thought these men would be swayed by the latest rage. They reminded Megan of her first stepfather. A practical man, he opted for what worked, not what other people thought would be best.

Red stared at Rita, a puzzled frown on his face. ''Why would we want anything from Italy?''

For once Rita had nothing to say.

''There are a lot of other choices,'' Adele assured Red, smiling.

''Good. Here. Try my coffee cake. It's a special recipe.'' Red handed Adele a plate with a slice of cake on it, then offered one to Megan and Rita. It only took one bite for Megan to know they were in good hands for the week. She looked up to find Chad watching her, and she corrected her thought. They were in good hands as far as food went. Imagining Chad's hands anywhere near her sent chills all over her body.

''This is delicious, Red,'' she hurriedly said.

''Glad you like it,'' the cook said, beaming as he passed around cups of coffee.

Chad slapped the man on the shoulders. ''Red, here, is a lot better cook than he ever was a cowboy.'' The men laughed, as if Chad's teasing was an old joke.

''Mr. Randall,'' Adele began, when Jake interrupted her.

"Make it 'Jake.' All of us answer to 'Mr. Randall.' It gets too confusing."

"Of course. Jake, how extensive are you wanting the plan we each present? Just a few rooms? The entire house? We'd like some guidelines."

Jake waved one hand to the room around him. "As extensive as you want to make it. The place hasn't had much done to it since our mother died more than twenty years ago. We're not big on socializing, so it hasn't really been a problem, but—but I think it's time we bring things up-to-date."

One of the other brothers stood abruptly, nodded to the ladies and muttered, "I need to get some work done," then left the room before anyone could say anything.

Jake frowned, and the other two looked uneasy. Chad cleared his throat. "Don't pay any attention to Pete's bad manners. He's got woman troubles."

"Don't pay any attention to Chad, either," Jake said, glaring at his brother. "As usual, he talks too much. Pete's starting a new business and has a lot on his mind."

Megan wondered what was going on between the brothers. Somehow Chad had displeased Jake.

"I'm servin' lunch in an hour. Best you take these ladies to their rooms," Red said, rounding up the dishes from their snack.

"Right," Jake agreed. "Brett, you and Chad take the ladies upstairs. If there's anything you need," Jake added, turning to them, "just let me know."

As they stood, murmuring polite responses, Chad appeared at Megan's side. "Right this way, Megan."

She was almost overcome with the urge to tell him her name was Miss Chase, but to deny him the familiarity Jake had offered them would be unspeakably rude. Besides, she was never standoffish. So why did she feel that way?

He took her arm, and Megan had the answer. Somehow this man threatened her serenity. A shiver engulfed her from his innocent touch. "Thank you," she said, and swiftly moved ahead of him.

Their luggage was waiting in the hall.

"If you'll each identify what's yours, we'll bring it to your rooms," Brett explained.

When Megan pointed out the two black pieces of luggage that belonged to her, Chad immediately picked them up.

"I can carry the smaller one," she insisted, reaching for the handle.

"Nope," Chad returned, one dark eyebrow slipping up. "I wouldn't dream of letting you do that. Here in Wyoming, we take care of our women."

Megan took a step back from him, holding back the urge to assure him she wasn't "his" woman. "But then you'll have to make two trips."

"We'll carry up yours and Adele's and come back for Rita's, since she brought more. It won't take us but a minute," Brett said. He was as handsome as his brother, but somehow Megan felt more at ease with Brett.

"Two of you will have to share a bath. The other room has its own. Does it matter to any of you?" Brett asked as he led the way up the stairs.

"I'll take the private bath," Rita quickly said, smirking at Adele and Megan.

When they reached the top of the stairs, Brett showed Rita to her room. "We'll bring your bags up in a minute."

The other two rooms were toward the front of the house. Chad led Megan to the room at the end of the hall, overlooking the porch.

Megan looked longingly at Brett and Adele, who were entering the room next door. She didn't want to be alone with Chad. Stepping into her room, she turned around and said, "Thank you. I can manage now."

Chad didn't seem ready to go, however. He carried the two bags across the room and set them down on a cedar chest. "Do you like the room?"

"It's very nice." She looked away from his brown eyes, hoping he'd leave while she could maintain her standoffish attitude. He was much too potent a package of male virility.

"You from Denver?"

"I live there now."

"But you weren't born there?"

"No." She walked to the front window, hoping he'd get the idea that she didn't want to talk.

"How long have you been a decorator?"

"Three years."

"Any boyfriends?"

Shocked by his sudden change of subject, she spun around to stare at him. "I beg your pardon?"

"Just checking to see if you were paying attention. You seemed a little distracted," he said with a self-assured smile. "But if you want to answer the question, I don't mind."

"No, thank you," she said, keeping her voice neutral.

"You don't like to give out too much information about yourself, do you?" He wandered across the room toward her.

What did she say now? No? That would be the truth. She cleared her throat. "I didn't realize you'd be interested."

He leaned against the windowsill and grinned at her. "Oh, yeah, I'm interested. We don't get such pretty visitors very often."

Then there must not be any women left in Wyoming. She couldn't imagine any other reason the Randall men would be suffering from loneliness.

When she said nothing, he moved a little closer. "Anything I can do to make your stay more... enjoyable, just let me know."

"Thank you, but I'll be busy working."

"All work and no play is bad." He reached out to finger the collar of her coat. "Besides, you might get lonesome."

She jerked away as his finger touched her cheek. She didn't know if she was misreading his offer or not, but she wanted to put an end to any ideas he seemed to have.

"Thank you for bringing up my bags, Mr. Randall. I'll try not to be a bother while I'm here."

Her deliberate formality had its effect. He straightened from his slouched position and stared at her, his gaze cool. "Oh, you'll be a bother, Miss Chase," he drawled, "one way or another. But I reckon we'll survive it." With a nod of his head, he left the room, and Megan sagged against the wall.

She only hoped *she* did.

CHAD WENT BACK DOWN the stairs for the other bags, a puzzled frown on his face. Megan Chase hadn't responded to his flirting at all. In fact, she'd seemed downright antagonistic. What had he done?

Not that it mattered, he hurriedly assured himself. After all, she wasn't the only beautiful woman in Wyoming. But there'd been something about her that drew his interest. Other than her looks, of course.

Brett was already picking up two of Rita's bags. "Where have you been? Chatting up the ladies?"

"Just being friendly. Left the two heaviest for me, didn't you?" he asked, noting the size of the bags.

"You're the youngest. We old folks have to be careful."

Since Brett was only three years older than Chad's twenty-six, he ignored his brother's dig.

"Besides, the lovely Rita will appreciate all your muscle. You'll probably be thanking me by the end of the day. She's definitely your type," Brett assured him as he started up the stairs.

Brett was right. Rita looked like the women he partied with occasionally at the bars in Casper. So why was he still thinking about Megan's reaction? There was no question about Rita's willingness to strike up a flirtation.

After escaping Rita's determined friendliness, Chad discovered his brothers all in the kitchen, sitting at the big table while Red prepared the meal.

"Aha! Here's our Romeo," Brett announced when he entered.

Jake sent Chad a sharp look.

"Cut it out, Brett," Chad protested at once. "Rita's on the prowl. I don't think she's too particular about who she catches as long as she catches someone." He pulled out a chair and sat down.

"That's not too gentlemanly a thing to say," Red criticized from the sink.

Chad shrugged. He figured if none of his brothers offered Rita their company, Red would have a good chance of getting lucky.

"So what do you think of them?" Jake asked. Chad noted his gaze went first to Pete.

"I guess they'll do a fine job," Brett answered first. "Though I don't think Red likes the idea of Italian tile."

"What do I need foreign stuff for?" Red demanded.

But Jake seemed to have no interest in a discussion of tile. "I'll expect everyone to clean up good for dinner each evening."

They all groaned.

"Damn," Brett groused, "it'll be like when the evil Chloe lived with us."

Chad noted the stricken look on Jake's face and felt for his brother, but Brett was right. These women were going to disturb their peace.

Jake turned to the one brother who'd remained silent. "Pete? What did you think of the decorators?"

Looking up from the column of figures he was adding, Pete gave his brother a puzzled look. "What?"

"The women. What did you think of them?"

Pete just shrugged his shoulders.

"I thought you liked blondes," Jake insisted. "Rita is pretty."

"If you like that type," Chad added. When his brothers, even Pete, turned to stare at him, he asked, "What?"

"Blondes are your speciality," Brett said, grinning. "You and Pete always go for the blondes. Have you changed your mind?"

Chad started to tell Brett he was leaning more toward light brown hair and hazel eyes, but he stopped himself. His brothers might recognize his description of Megan Chase, and he didn't want them thinking either of the ladies mattered. Not to him. He never let women interfere with his life.

"Variety is always good," he said, shrugging his shoulders like Pete.

"I guess you haven't changed, after all," Brett teased, and they all laughed.

The conversation reminded Chad of something else. "By the way, Rita is already asking about nightlife. I told her I'd ask you if you'd planned something," he added, looking at Jake.

"I hadn't really planned anything. I thought we'd show them the ranch, things like that. You'll help out, won't you, Pete?" Jake asked.

"I don't have time for that, Jake. The vet is coming soon to look at the house we've set aside for him. And I've got—"

"Hey, a good idea, Pete. You need to show the decorators that house. They might have some ideas for fixing it up. Why don't you do that this afternoon?" Jake stood. "Yeah. That's a good plan. I'll explain to the ladies over lunch."

Before Pete, staring at his brother openmouthed, could complain, Jake left the room.

"What's got into him?" Pete demanded, staring at the other three. "He knows I'm trying to start my new business. You two are sitting around doing nothing, and he picks on me."

Chad was wondering the same thing. Oh, not that he and Brett were doing nothing, but the winter months were their less active period.

A sudden reason occurred to him. "Maybe Jake thinks you need a little cheering up since Janie's—" He stopped right there as Pete sent him a steely look that warned him he might have his nose broken again if he continued.

Pete shoved back his chair. "You can handle the social hour, little brother. That'll teach you to mind your tongue." He stomped out of the room toward the back porch, the opposite direction from Jake.

"Whew! That was close," Brett said. "You ought to know better than to mention Janie's name."

"Damn it, she's an old friend. I went to school with her. Just because Pete and her parted doesn't mean I can't even say her name."

Brett grinned at Chad. "Then I'd up my medical insurance if I were you. Come to think of it, when Jake finds out Pete dumped his guide role on you, you may be in trouble all over again."

"Why is Jake wanting Pete to spend time with the women? I thought he might be interested in one of them himself, but now I'm not so sure."

Brett shrugged, but Red agreed with Chad's earlier theory. "I think you got the right of it, boy. Pete's not been the same lately. I think Jake's tryin' to cheer him up."

"I don't think it's working," Chad said.

"Maybe not, but these ladies are going to do wonders for your social life," Brett teased. "Seems to me, for all your talk, you've been slipping lately. You stayed home last night—on a Saturday night!"

"There were snowstorm warnings," Chad said defensively. He'd been going into town less and less lately, and that fact bothered him. Was he getting old? Losing interest in women? It wasn't a good sign when a book held more excitement than a warm, willing woman.

A mental picture of Megan Chase immediately reassured him. No, he hadn't given up women. Maybe he was becoming more particular in his old age.

"You boys better go get cleaned up for lunch," Red warned. "I'm ringing the bell in five minutes."

When Chad returned to the kitchen a few minutes later, everyone except Pete was already at the table.

"You're late," Jake declared. Before Chad could round the table and take the seat beside Megan, Jake gestured to the empty place between Brett and Adele. "Come join Adele, Chad. She attended the University of Wyoming, too."

Chad wasn't sure what he would have in common with the lady who had attended his alma mater, since she was old enough to be his mother, but he obeyed Jake. Besides, that chair put him across the table from Megan, where he could see her much better.

He grinned at her. All she did was look away. What had he done? Had he offended her in some way? Rita, on the other hand, made a point of greeting him.

"I was afraid you weren't going to join us for lunch, Chad," she purred.

"I don't miss many meals, ma'am," he assured her, but he kept his gaze on Megan.

For several minutes, everyone was silent as they passed the dishes around. Chad couldn't help noticing the polite strain that filled the air. It was in such contrast to their normally noisy meals. Women complicated life. And that was why he shouldn't be interested in the woman across from him.

But he was.

He looked at Megan again. She acted as if he didn't even exist. He didn't like being ignored. Leaning forward, he asked, "How do you like Red's cooking, Megan?"

Not looking at Chad, Megan turned to Red. "The food is delicious, Red."

The old man grinned with pleasure.

Chad ground his teeth. And tried again. "Ever been on a ranch before?"

"Yes," she replied, no warmth in her voice. And she kept her eyes on her plate.

"I haven't," Rita enthused.

Chad had to endure several minutes of vapid conversation from the blonde before he could try again. "You're not a city girl, Megan?"

Her hazel eyes brushed over him, sending unexpected chills over him. She pushed a silky strand of hair behind one ear, and the urge to trace the path of her fingers was undeniable.

Jake interrupted his thoughts. "This afternoon you ladies will take a look at a nearby house. A new vet is going to move in, and I wouldn't mind a few suggestions about fixing it up."

Despite the repercussions, Chad was happy he'd traded the job of tour guide with Pete. He'd get to spend more time with Megan. Just the thought of getting her alone in the barn filled him with anticipation—and a feeling he hesitated to name....

He had to get a grip on these fantasies, he admonished. Or else—like Jake with Chloe—he'd find himself in a heap of trouble.

Chapter Three

"Well, that's the nickel tour," Chad announced to the three women. "Anyone want the dollar version through the barns?"

The smell of hay always invoked happy memories of Megan's years on her stepfather's ranch, and in spite of her vow to avoid Chad, she immediately agreed. "Oh, yes, I'd love to see the barns."

"If it won't offend you, Chad," Adele said, "I'll return to the house. I'm not the outdoor type."

Chad grinned. "Of course I don't mind. Not everyone is agreeable to getting manure on their shoes."

Rita had moved to Chad's side, taking his arm again, but she stepped away at his words. "What? You mean there is actually such disgusting stuff in your barns?"

"The barns are where we keep our best animals during cold weather, Rita," Chad explained.

"But doesn't someone clean it up?"

He stiffened as if she'd impugned his honor. "Yes, ma'am, every day."

Rita looked down at her expensive heels and then glared at Megan. Before leaving the house, Megan had changed into wool pants and loafers.

"You'd better come back to the house with me," Adele said. "You're not dressed for a trip to the barn. I'm sure Chad will show it to you later."

After sending another antagonistic look Megan's way, Rita turned to Chad. "Will you give me a personal tour later, Chad?"

"We can probably work it in," he said, but Megan noticed he didn't meet Rita's gaze.

It amused her that Chad, whom she'd already classified as a consummate flirt, had more than met his match in Rita. He was backing away as fast as he could without tripping over his boots.

"Then I'll see you later," Rita said, patting his arm and batting her lashes at him.

Megan was so amused with Rita's antics, it didn't occur to her that she, too, was going to receive a personal tour until Rita and Adele opened the door.

"Wait! I'll go back with you. There's no need for Chad to waste his time showing me the barns now. I'll see them some other time."

Chad grabbed her arm as she headed for the door. "No problem. I don't have anything else I need to do. You two go ahead."

There wasn't anything Megan could say now without sending up a flag saying she didn't want to be alone with Chad Randall. And she wasn't willing to expose her fears to the man. So she just nodded to Adele.

"Yes, go ahead. I'll be back at the house soon."

Chad held her beside him until the door closed behind the other two, as if he were afraid she'd change her mind at the last minute. Then he released her.

"Well, shall we go?" she hurriedly asked, moving toward the door.

"There's no hurry. I'd rather get to know you."

He moved closer, and Megan remembered how he'd touched her cheek in her room earlier. The last thing she needed was to get close to one of the Randall men.

"I'm not very interesting. How many barns do you have?"

"Lady, you don't understand men if you think you wouldn't stand out, even in a crowd." With his words came a sexy smile that sent shivers over her.

He just wouldn't get the message. Turning toward the door, she asked over her shoulder, "Which way?"

A large hand closed around her upper arm. "Now, darlin', don't be in such a hurry. We've got plenty of time."

His touch only confirmed what she'd already discovered. This man was potent, one who would encourage any woman to lose her head. She pulled from his grasp. "Stop!"

"Stop what?" he asked, a frown replacing his flirtatious grin.

"Stop playing games."

"Games?" he questioned, one eyebrow rising to emphasize his puzzlement. "What do you mean?"

She wished she hadn't decided to be honest. But it was too late now. "I'm talking about your flirting."

His brown eyes narrowed. "You been talking to my brothers?"

"No, I haven't. I don't have to ask anyone." She gestured in the direction Rita had gone. "I've seen you in action. You certainly wouldn't act like this if I were a man."

"I *hope* not," he responded with a grin. "If I flirted with a man, my reputation would be ruined!"

"I didn't mean that, and you know it!" she exclaimed in frustration. "But I'm here as a professional, not as your date."

He took another step closer. "Just because you're here to do a job doesn't mean we can't be friendly. I haven't had any complaints from other 'friends.'"

"I'm sure you haven't, but I'm not interested."

"You already got a man?"

Megan blew out her breath in frustration. "Is that all you think I meant? Must I have a man if I don't fall at your feet? You certainly have a large ego, don't you?"

He moved closer to her, and she backed to the wall. "You think you know all about me in one afternoon?"

She raised her chin. "I think you expect women to play along with you. Look at what you're doing now. You're cornering me, using your strength, your size, against me."

His eyes widened as if surprised by what she'd said. "I'm not— Well, maybe it seems that way. But what if I just wanted to be close to you?"

"Don't you think I should have some say in that decision?"

CHAD HAD NEVER THOUGHT about the woman's point of view. He'd never had to. The women he'd spent time with invited his closeness.

Damn it, she was right! He had pressed her against the wall, without ever touching her. And he knew she didn't want him close to her. He felt like a heel, and he didn't like it. "Come on," he growled as he turned away. "Let's go see the barns."

He wasn't sure she'd come. Opening the door, he stood back and waited. If she hightailed it back to the house, he wouldn't stop her.

"Are you sure you don't mind?" she asked again after he closed the door to the house.

"I said I didn't."

"But that was before I—"

"Look, contrary to your opinion, I've heard the word *no* before. Let's go."

He watched out of the corner of his eye as she tugged her overcoat closer around her. Megan Chase had Rita beat all hollow in the looks department. She wasn't flashy, but there was a sheen, a polish, to her that gave the impression of pure gold.

"How many barns do you have?" she asked again.

Chad noticed she was almost running to keep up with him, and he slowed down. "Four. Actually one of them is an indoor arena."

"An indoor arena? You mean like a rodeo?"

He grinned reluctantly at the enthusiasm in her voice. "Yeah, sort of. You like rodeos?" This Megan, eager and smiling, was more enjoyable than the antagonistic one he'd just faced.

"Yes, though I haven't been to all that many."

"And you aren't worried about the mistreatment of all those animals?" His grin widened as she recognized his mocking of one of Rita's earlier inane statements.

"Shame on you!" she said with a laugh, the first time she'd relaxed in his presence.

He wanted to kiss her. That thought stopped him in his tracks. She'd just pushed him away, told him to get lost and he wanted to kiss her. Real bad.

"What? Did I offend you?" she asked, stopping when she realized he wasn't keeping up with her.

"Nope. I just thought of something. You want to see the arena first?" He automatically took her arm and then paused again. "Is this all right?"

She looked at him, surprised. "Of course. You're just guiding me in the right direction, aren't you?"

"Yeah, but I'm touching you." *And liking it.*

Her cheeks flushed. "But it's out of courtesy, not— not a come-on."

"Oh. I guess I got confused." And still was. If Megan thought he could touch her and not have a sexual response, she was naive. Right now he was fighting the urge to pull her into his embrace.

He released her arm when they reached the arena. She eagerly entered the building, her gaze darting all around. Her interest seemed to be real.

The main area of the barn consisted of a large corral where the cowboys could practice their skills even when the ground was covered in snow. At the moment, several men were training some cow ponies in the art of cutting out cattle.

Megan crossed her arms over the top rail and propped her foot on the bottom one as naturally as if she'd been raised on a ranch.

"You like horses?" he asked, keeping his voice casual. She seemed reluctant to share anything about herself, but he hoped if she didn't notice his questions, she'd be more forthcoming.

"Yes," she said, but her gaze remained on the horses in the corral.

"Ever owned one?"

"Yeah. Jim gave me a sorrel mare. I named her Baby Doll," she added, grimacing at him as if daring him to criticize her choice.

He was more concerned with the identity of Jim than he was with her choice of names. An unexpected surge of jealousy filled him. To put her at ease, he said, "I named my first one Blackie. Not too imaginative."

She acknowledged his comment with a smile and looked at the work going on in the corral again.

"Who's Jim?"

"My stepfather," she murmured. "Wow! Did you see that move?"

"Yeah." Stepfather. Chad took a deep breath of relief before asking another question, but the cowboys stopped work and rode over to the rail.

After introductions and a little talk, Chad said goodbye and led Megan to the next barn. "We keep the mares ready to foal in here," he explained, then stood back to watch Megan make friends with his horses. She was a natural, he decided, stroking the mares, crooning to them.

"So, do you still have Baby Doll?"

A sad look crossed her face. "No."

"What happened?"

"I moved away," she said in clipped tones, and walked to the next stall. The mare occupying it was a favorite of Chad's.

"Let me introduce you to Maybelle," he said, pretending he hadn't noticed her terseness. "And in the corner is the latest addition to the ranch, her baby." He scratched the animal's forehead while Megan leaned over the half gate to see the foal.

"Oh, it's beautiful. A filly or a colt?"

"A filly. Want to name her?"

She whirled around, a gleam of excitement in her eyes. "Doesn't she have a name already?"

"Nope. She was just born last night."

"But your brothers might not like my choice."

"Doesn't matter. Maybelle belongs to me. What's a good name for the little lady?" He leaned against the gate and watched the delight on her face. It made him feel good all over.

"Oh, I think she should be named— No, you'd hate it."

"How will I know until you tell me?"

"I just thought—she's tiny. Would you consider 'Tinkerbell' too silly?"

He would have agreed to any name to receive that smile from Megan, but he considered 'Tinkerbell' more than appropriate. Matching her smile, he said, "I like it."

"You do? I would've thought you'd want something more . . . serious." She watched his face for a reaction, as if she didn't believe his earlier agreement.

"Serious? When her mother's name is Maybelle? What did you expect, National Velvet?"

"Did you watch that movie? I saw it when I was small, and I loved it," Megan said, still smiling.

He liked this Megan so much more than the earlier one, who put him in his place. "Yeah, I saw that movie. In fact, I think we have a copy of it. Dad bought us one of the first VCRs and started building a film library. It comes in handy when we're snowed in with nothing to do."

"Do you get snowed in often?"

"Yeah," he told her with a laugh. "In fact, the weather we've been having the past couple of days is rare. I think you brought Denver's weather with you. Beautiful weather and a beautiful woman. Jake got a real bargain."

The smile immediately disappeared, and she gave him a cold stare before walking toward the door of the barn.

"Megan? What's wrong?"

"I'm ready to go back to the house."

"I can tell. But I don't understand why."

"I told you I'm not interested in flirting."

"Flirting? Flirting includes an honest compliment? Are you telling me you don't know you're beautiful?" He couldn't keep incredulity from his voice. "Or that men haven't told you how beautiful you are?"

"You're exaggerating," she said huffily, standing by the door, waiting for him to join her.

He strolled over to her, determined not to apologize for thinking her beautiful. "Lady, you don't take a compliment well, do you?"

"I guess not. So you should forget about paying me any more."

Gone was the laughing, relaxed young woman who'd named his newest filly and talked about her own horse. Instead, the stiff, formal Megan was beside him again.

He swung open the door and waited for her to go back out into the cold sunshine, then followed her. "I'll try to keep that in mind," he muttered, irritation filling him.

Though the sun was shining, there was almost a foot of snow on the ground. The path had been cleared between the barn and the house, but it was narrow.

Chad slammed the barn door to relieve his frustration, and the noise must have startled Megan because she tripped over the mound of snow next to the cleared path and went sprawling into it.

He grabbed her arm and tugged her back to her feet. "Are you all right?"

Snow was caked on her coat and even in her hair. He began brushing her off.

"D-don't," she protested, shoving his hands away.

"I'm just trying to help," he protested, continuing to remove the snow.

She backed away and again fell, this time on her back. "What are you doing to me?" she yelled at him. "Trying to turn me into a snowman?"

He pulled her to her feet again. "You wouldn't have fallen if you'd stood still. Now you've got snow all over you."

"I can—"

"Hold still!" he roared, his patience at an end. "If I take you into the house like this, Jake will have my hide."

Finally she followed his orders and allowed him to brush her off. When he ran a hand through her hair, he saw uneasiness fill her eyes, but she didn't move—until she suddenly squealed and leapt forward into his arms, knocking him into the snow on the other side of the path and falling on top of him.

Chad lay there stunned until her warm, squirming body on top of him got his attention. He'd better get her off him fast before she felt how attracted he was to her. Without warning, he dumped her sideways in the snow.

"Lady, do you *want* to die of pneumonia?"

"No! Of course not!"

"Then do you mind explaining what happened? First you don't want me to touch you, and then you leap into my arms."

She struggled to a sitting position. "I didn't leap into your arms," she assured him indignantly. "Some snow fell onto my neck and—and it shocked me. I didn't intend to—I'm sorry." She struggled to her feet, again covered with snow. "Aren't you going to get up?"

"I don't know. Are you sure it's safe?" He stared up at her, wishing he could pull her back down against him.

Something in his eyes must've given his thoughts away. She backed toward the house.

"Wait," he called as he got up. "I still can't let you go back to the house covered with snow. I don't want Jake to think I mistreated you."

"It's all right," she said, moving farther away. "I'll explain that I fell."

"That won't satisfy Jake. Come on, Megan. It won't take but a minute." Since she stopped moving, he assumed she accepted his words. He began the process of removing the snow all over again, turning her back to him and brushing her derriere gently. Then her back and, with a warning, her hair.

His fingers tangled in the silky strands, now a little damp, and grazed her warm neck beneath them. Heat surged through him. Spinning her around, he discovered she'd been working on the front of her coat and it was almost clear. Damn. Too bad. He'd been looking forward to covering that territory.

"You have some snow on you, too," she said, surprising him. "Turn around."

Automatically he did as she asked. But as her hands slid over his backside, he realized her touching him wasn't a good idea. Even through his jeans, he felt her fingers. Or maybe he just had a good imagination.

Whirling back around, he had to reach out to grab her arms as his abrupt movement had her losing her balance all over again. "No, you don't! Not again."

She surprised him, bursting into laughter, her hazel eyes sparkling above flushed cheeks.

Adorable.

And irresistible. Almost with a will of their own, his hands pulled her against him and his lips touched the softness of hers.

He didn't intend to deepen the kiss, to plead for her to open her lips to his. He was sure he didn't. But somehow, before he even realized it was happening, her arms were around his neck and her curves were pressed into his flesh.

Just as he decided he'd found heaven, that nothing could be sweeter than Megan's lips, she wrenched her mouth away from his and gave a mighty shove. The next thing he knew, both of them were sitting in the snow. Again.

"You—you—" Megan sputtered, glaring at him. "See? I told you! You're a flirt!"

"You didn't exactly stop me!" he roared back at her, frustration filling him.

"Of course! That's just like a man! Blame me for *your* behavior."

"Hey! That's not what— Wait, Megan!" he suddenly called as she got to her feet and stomped toward the house.

He jumped up and set off in hot pursuit, but she'd gotten a head start. "Wait! Let me dust off the snow."

"I don't care if I look like Frosty the Snowman," she said between clenched teeth, "I wouldn't let you touch me again."

He was only a step behind her as she rushed through the back door. Just close enough to realize their entrance was going to be observed by his brothers.

Megan seemed unaware of their audience until she came to a screeching halt two steps into the room.

Unfortunately Chad wasn't able to put on the brakes quite as soon and bumped into her, his arms automatically coming around her.

She angrily pushed him away just as Jake spoke.

"Hi, Megan. Did you—? What the hell happened to you?"

Chapter Four

"You made a pass at Megan?" Jake demanded, frowning ferociously at Chad, making him want to slink down in the chair.

After his and Megan's abrupt entry to the kitchen, Chad had known he'd have some explaining to do. Jake hadn't bought the falling-down-in-the-snow story Megan had lamely offered. An actress she wasn't.

Jake had ordered Chad to his office.

"Not exactly." He hadn't intended it as a pass. It had just...happened.

"Why don't you tell me what occurred on your little tour? You obviously dumped the other two. They turned up back here over an hour ago."

"I didn't dump them. They decided they didn't want to see the barns. But Megan did. So I gave her the extended tour." He sounded defensive and decided to try another tack. "Look, Jake, I didn't intend any— It just happened!"

"What I want to know is just exactly what 'it' is."

Jake's steely glare reminded Chad of a few other sessions in his big brother's office. Jake had taken on his father's duties frequently, especially where his brothers were concerned.

"I kissed her."

"And then buried her in snow?"

"No! First she fell down and—and then she fell down again. I was trying to brush her off and we both fell and—and I kissed her."

"That's all?"

"Word of honor." Chad breathed a sigh of relief when Jake nodded. His brother's trust was important to him.

"Well, you can't do that anymore."

Wondering if he'd heard right, Chad stared at Jake. "What did you say?"

"You heard me. I don't want you messing around with Megan."

Chad's earlier suspicions resurfaced. Was Jake interested in Megan? "Why?"

"I can't explain right now. But tonight, after dinner, you follow along with my plans. And keep your thoughts on Rita. She's much more your type." With that, Jake strode from the office.

Damn. Chad was getting tired of everyone telling him Rita was his type. He could pick up a woman like Rita any day of the week. But Megan... He abruptly halted his straying thoughts.

Jake didn't ask much of him. And it wasn't as if he had any serious thoughts about Megan. After all, marriage wasn't something he ever contemplated, and Megan would be gone back to Denver before he could do much more than— He'd better stop right there. If he thought about touching her, kissing her . . .

He sprang up from the chair as if he'd had a shock. Time to occupy his mind with work. Not a certain hazel-eyed beauty who could drive him crazy in no time at all.

AFTER DINNER that evening, when Rita wanted to know what entertainment was available, Chad discovered Jake's plan. Chad and Brett were assigned the task of watching a movie with Rita while Pete and Jake played forty-two, a domino game, with Adele and Megan.

Since Pete didn't looked thrilled with the prospect of dominos, Chad hurriedly offered to switch places.

"That's generous of you, little brother, but I think Pete will enjoy the game." The tone of Jake's voice told Chad he wasn't pleased.

"Sure. Just thought I'd offer." When Rita threaded her arm through his, Chad gave her a jaunty smile, as if she'd just fulfilled his life's dream, but out of the corner of his eye, he watched for Megan's reaction.

Nothing.

"What movie shall we watch?" Rita asked.

"Whatever you want," he replied, and reluctantly led her down the hall.

MEGAN BREATHED a sigh of relief as Chad and Rita left the kitchen. She'd done her best to ignore the irritating man ever since they'd gotten back to the house and made their embarrassing entry.

She'd also tried to put their kiss out of her head. But anytime she got within ten feet of Chad Randall, a tingling surged all through her. And she wanted to throw herself into his arms.

"Ridiculous!" she muttered.

"What did you say?" Pete asked as they walked to the living room.

"I said I love forty-two." And that was the only thing she was going to love. It wasn't just that she was wary of charming, flirtatious men because of her latest stepfather's roving eye. No, Megan had seen it all firsthand—from her very own fiancé.

While he was engaged *to* her, he was also engaged *with* other women—in secret little rendezvouses. Lucky for her they weren't all kept hush-hush and she'd found out just what kind of man he was *before* she walked down the aisle to him.

Her mother hadn't been as lucky, nor had she learned from her mistakes. And Megan had spent her life shuffling from one stepfather to another. But when her mother had married the rancher in Colorado, Megan had become part of a large family for the first time in her life. She'd been in heaven. For four years.

Then her mother had packed their bags and took her away. She'd never been able to recapture that elusive feeling of being part of a family—and now she envied

Chad for his loving brothers. But once Megan had gained control of her life, she'd vowed she'd never again offer her heart to anyone. And that included Chad Randall.

"I'm glad you like the game. 'Cause we play to win around here." Pete's wicked chuckle interrupted her thoughts. "The last time I lost to Jake, he had me rubbing down his horse for a week."

"Then I wouldn't mind losing. I'd love to be around horses again."

"You like to ride?" Jake said from behind her.

"I love it. I'd love to try some of the cutting horses I saw in the barn today."

"That can be arranged if you want to meet me in the barn in the morning," Jake said. "Pete and I will put you through your paces."

"That would be great!" Anything to keep her mind off another Randall and his wickedly sexy kiss.

An hour later, the hair on the back of her neck stood on end, and she turned around to discover Chad standing in the door of the room watching her.

"Movie over?" Jake asked.

"Nope. Red told me to ask if you're ready for some chocolate cake."

Megan heard him move closer, but she refused to look at him again. She couldn't. Slapping her domino down on the table, she looked at Pete instead. The startled expression on his face had her looking at her domino again. "Pete, I'm sorry," she said with a groan. She'd out-trumped her own partner.

"No problem," Pete responded with a smile, carefully hiding his true reaction.

There was only one more round of play, and they made their bid. Then Jake pushed back his chair. "Maybe it's time for a break. This game can get a little tense."

Megan felt about two inches high. They were kindly making excuses for her boner play. "Pete might like a change of partners, as well as a piece of cake."

As the two older Randall brothers protested, Chad spoke up. "Maybe Rita would like to play."

Adele, who hadn't said anything, leaned forward. "It would be my guess that Rita has never heard of the game, much less want to play it."

"Good," Pete said, slipping an arm around Megan as they all stood. " 'Cause I wouldn't want to change partners. We're in the lead."

Chad glared at both her and Pete, and Megan looked away.

When they finished their dessert and returned to play, Megan was able to relax. Chad had been banished to the movie again. Indeed, Jake had ordered him to return to Rita and Brett.

Before Megan could think about that fact, the game began and she was determined she wouldn't embarrass her partner again. As a testament to her concentration, and maybe a little luck, they ended the game an hour later with her and Pete declared the winners.

"Good job, Megan!" Pete exclaimed. "I think I'll have Jake ride fences this week as payment."

"You're going to get your pound of flesh, aren't you?" Jake said with a wry grin that Megan found charming.

In fact, all the brothers were charming. Warm-hearted, polite, with a generous sense of humor, they were the answer to any woman's prayer. Even more attractive to Megan was the love the four men shared with no embarrassment.

She'd wanted to be part of a big family all her life. In Colorado she'd had that feeling for a short while. She knew that craving for connections lurked deep within her. Another reason to avoid the Randalls. She couldn't trust herself.

"I'll ride fences with you, Jake," Megan offered.

"You really do want to ride, don't you?" Jake said with a laugh. "No need to be so sacrificial, Megan. You can ride in the indoor arena. In winter it's the best bet."

"You've got a deal. If you'll excuse me, I think I'll go up to bed now."

"How about a cup of hot cocoa before you go upstairs?" Pete offered.

"No, thanks." She wanted to be safely in her room before the movie ended.

She started up the stairs, deep in thought. Jake and Pete were wonderful. Why did they not affect her the way Chad did?

She rounded the corner at the top of the stairs and gasped as she bumped into a broad, muscular chest.

Chad's arms went around her, and she found herself in a repeat of their snowy encounter.

But this time, when she pushed away from him, her feet didn't go out from under her. "Excuse me," she murmured, and tried to go around him.

"Wait a minute. Are you through playing?"

"Yes."

"How about something to drink? We could go to the kitchen and—"

"No!" She drew a deep breath and tempered her response. "Thank you, but I'm tired." Again she tried to go around him. He shifted his large body to intercept her.

"Listen, Megan, I wanted to tell you that I'm sorry for what happened earlier."

His words were all that was polite. The look in his eyes started her to trembling. The fire she could see there stirred the coals of her attraction to the man... and her memory of his touch. "Thanks," she managed to choke out.

"Normally I wouldn't treat a guest like that."

"Okay." He still didn't move to let her pass.

"It was the close proximity that caused—"

"I see. I should keep my distance, is that it?" She hadn't wanted the embrace, but she resented his explaining it away with "proximity."

"Well, I only meant—"

"You've made your meaning quite clear. I'll warn Adele and Rita to keep their distance, too, unless they want to be mauled." She regretted her choice of words at once, but refused to admit it. Shoving against his arm, this time she succeeded in bypassing the sexiest blockade she'd ever seen.

"Ow!"

Chad stared in shock at the blood oozing from the cut on his hand.

"What happened?" Brett asked, looking over the back of the horse he was saddling.

"I cut myself on a piece of barbed wire some fool left laying about!" Chad shouted, anger at himself filling him. He hadn't been paying attention, or he would've noticed the wire hung over the bench.

Brett came around his horse and took Chad's hand, examining it. "Doesn't look too bad. You'd better go let Red look at it, though."

Chad wasn't about to go back in the house. He didn't want to chance facing Megan. Last night was enough. The upstairs hallway had felt colder than the barn this morning. "It's okay. Where's that first-aid kit we keep in the barns?"

With a dryness that called Chad to order, Brett said, "Where it always is. What's wrong with you this morning?"

"I guess I had my mind on other things." If a man could call Megan Chase a "thing." A major distraction. A teenager would call her a hot babe. That would do.

"Chad? Chad!"

He turned to his brother with a frown. What was he yelling for? "Yeah?"

"Hey, bro, you'd better clear your head before we mount up. You're going to get both of us in trouble if you don't." While he was talking, Brett had fetched the first-aid kit and now began to clean the gash.

Chad cringed with Brett's rough treatment. "Maybe I should've gone to Red after all. Red wouldn't be so rough."

"So why didn't you?"

Brett's brown-eyed gaze, like his own, stared and Chad had to look away. "No need to disturb anyone."

"Uh-huh. Seems to me you might find several angels of mercy just waiting to bandage you."

His brother's remarks were too close to the bone. Chad jerked his hand away. "I can handle it from here."

"Hold still and don't act any dumber than you are." Brett's grin took the sting out of his words, and Chad obeyed. Brett unwrapped a bandage and covered the cut. "That ought to keep it clean for a while at least. We'll take a couple of these with us."

Once they were in the saddle, hats pulled low and coats zipped high, Brett asked another question. "What do you think's going on?"

Chad looked sharply at his brother and then let his gaze roam over the snow-covered range. "What do you mean?"

"You know what I mean. These women. If all Jake wanted was a new paint job and some furniture, he wouldn't bring in three women from Denver. And he sure as hell wouldn't give half his time to entertaining them."

"Maybe he's feeling the isolation this winter. Things have changed since Dad's death."

"Do you think Jake is thinking of remarrying?"

A coldness filled Chad. He'd shied away from thinking about Jake's order to leave Megan alone. It didn't much matter why if Jake asked something from him. But the idea of Jake and Megan . . . Chad shut down his wayward thoughts.

He cleared his throat. "Uh, I don't know. What do you think?"

Brett shrugged his shoulders. "I think we can eliminate Adele. She's a nice lady, but a bit long in the tooth for any of us. And Rita is too obvious to be believed. That leaves the lovely Megan."

"And?" Chad said harshly, anxious to hear what Brett had to say.

"Well, I think either he's interested in Megan, or he wants Pete to be. After all, you and I were sent to babysit Rita."

"Maybe he was just trying to be a good host." Even to Chad, his remark didn't have much merit. He wasn't surprised when Brett chuckled.

"Yeah, right."

They rode on in silence. Chad's thoughts lingered on the attraction he felt for Megan Chase before he considered the other part of the equation. Jake and Pete were family. They'd been surrogate fathers, as well as brothers. He could sacrifice a little pleasure—maybe a lot of pleasure—if either of them was interested in Megan.

Couldn't he?

CHAD FIGURED he had his answer. Jake had invited the three decorators out to a steak dinner in Rawhide, the nearest town. He'd also made it clear, one way or another, that Rita was Chad's responsibility tonight, while Pete would take care of Megan.

That meant it was Pete whom Jake had in mind for Megan. And it looked as if his plan was working. On the way to the restaurant, Pete and Megan kept their heads together, talking so quietly he couldn't hear a word they said. Especially not with Rita chattering away incessantly.

When they reached the restaurant, he managed to maneuver himself next to Megan.

"What were you and Pete talking about?" he asked her. It was the first time he'd spoken to her since their meeting in the hallway last night.

She raised one eyebrow. "Why?"

"Just curious. Pete's not much of a talker."

"So he said."

The waitress passed out menus and told them the night's specials. Megan leaned toward Pete and asked him what he recommended, and Chad clenched his jaw. She was ignoring him.

"Chad, sweetie, what should I order?" Rita crooned. "You know what a small appetite I have."

"Have a salad." He didn't care what she ate as long as it kept her from bothering him.

Several men stopped by the table to greet the three Randalls, but Chad wasn't misled by their friendliness. Three new women, all of them good-looking, even if Adele was older, stirred a lot of interest in their neck of the woods. He could tell by Jake's frown that he wasn't too pleased about the circling of the wolves, either.

"People are very friendly here," Megan said after a third group had left the table.

Pete snorted with smothered laughter. "Yeah, that they are. But they're not as friendly when it's just us Randalls, you know."

"Wait until we get to the dancing," Jake added gloomily. "They'll be all over us."

"How wonderful," Rita enthused, ignoring the Randalls' unhappiness. "I love to dance."

A little over an hour later, Jake's prediction came true. The minute the band began warming up, several men drifted over to their table to extend invitations to dance. Jake told them all to back off until the Randalls had a few dances with the ladies.

There was a lot of laughter in the room, and even Pete seemed more relaxed than Chad had seen him in a long time. Why shouldn't he be? He had Megan beside him. Chad tried to dismiss his jealous thoughts, but he couldn't keep his gaze from Megan.

The first dance began, and Chad, after Pete led Megan out on the dance floor, took Rita's hand.

He scarcely noticed when Rita pressed against him. He was too busy watching Megan dancing at a discreet distance from Pete. She was a good dancer, with a natural rhythm.

"Chad? Did you hear me?"

"Um, no, Rita. What did you say?"

"I wanted to know how long the band will play. Until midnight?"

"I don't know." He hoped not. It was going to be a long night. At least he knew Rita would have a lot of offers to dance. That would leave him free. He could have at least one dance with Megan. That would be expected of him. To do otherwise would be impolite. He was sure Jake would understand. He'd wait awhile, bide his time. He didn't want to seem too anxious.

Pete and Megan moved away from them, and Chad swung Rita in that direction so abruptly that she protested. "Sorry," he apologized, but he didn't drop his pursuit of the other two.

When the music stopped, he managed to be right next to Pete and Megan. The earlier decision to wait seemed silly when the opportunity presented itself. His rationale couldn't quite disguise the raging need to touch her again. "Shall we change partners?" he suggested casually to his brother.

"Sure," Pete said gallantly, extending his hand to Rita.

Chad gathered Megan into his arms with a hunger that disturbed him. She was just a woman. He didn't *need* her. But she was the perfect size, her head coming just above his chin. He leaned his cheek against her silky hair and inhaled a delicate, flowery scent.

"Nice perfume," he murmured.

She pulled back and looked up at him. "Thank you. It's gardenias."

"And you," he added with a smile.

"And me," she agreed. "Is this place always so crowded?"

"There aren't too many other places to go. You must dance a lot."

"Why?"

"'Cause you're good." He dared pull her a little closer, reveling in the feel of her soft curves against him.

"My mother insisted on dancing lessons. She thought that skill was much more important than something that would provide me with a job."

"And what did your father teach you?" he asked, hardly even realizing what he'd said until she stiffened.

"That happiness doesn't last."

He pulled back and looked down at her. "Your parents are divorced?"

"No. He didn't come back from Vietnam."

"And your mother remarried."

"Yes."

She was as tightly strung as a new barbed-wire fence. "You don't like your stepfather?"

"My newest stepfather, the fourth since my father died, is only ten years older than me. I consider him to be a gigolo. No, I don't like him." Her voice had tightened with each word.

"Sorry. Bad subject, I guess," he whispered, tucking her head to his shoulder.

She didn't let her head rest there. "It doesn't matter."

Something about the tone of her voice now and the way it had sounded earlier, when they'd argued at the foreman's house, made his eyes narrow. "Is your stepfather a flirt?"

"The worst."

He pulled back from her again. "You weren't comparing me to him, were you?"

Watching her gaze, he knew when she figured out his question, and her cheeks flushed. "You were flirting."

"Not like a gigolo," he protested.

"Flirting is flirting."

"Lady, you've got a lot to learn."

"Probably, but you're not going to be the one to teach me." She stiffened in his arms, her body no longer pliant.

"You're thinking Pete will? Listen, Pete's had a hard time. Don't give him any more heartache." She'd upset him with her words, but he hadn't meant to talk about Pete's personal business. He wished he could take the words back.

"What do you mean?"

"Nothing."

They finished the dance in silence, Megan stiff and tense in his arms. He regretted their entire conversation. If he'd paid attention to Jake's plan, he wouldn't have asked her to dance and then—and then he wouldn't have held her against him again.

As soon as the music ended, she pulled away from him and hurried back to the table. Before she could sit down, however, she was surrounded by eager cowboys.

Chad joined his two brothers as the music started again. All three ladies were on the dance floor.

"You okay?" Jake asked.

Chad managed a smile. "Sure. Looks like we won't have to worry about dancing our feet off."

"True," Pete agreed. "And I was worried."

"You didn't want to dance with Megan?" Jake asked, a frown on his face.

"Dancing with Megan was fine. I might not even mind dancing with Adele. It's Rita I'm staying away from."

"Well, she'll be real popular tonight, then. I just hope she doesn't upset anyone bad enough to fight."

"It's too nice a night to do any fighting," Pete assured his brother, leaning back in his chair and watching the dancers.

Chad watched them, too, wondering if he should ask Megan to dance again. Actually he knew he shouldn't. But he wanted to. When the music ended, he rose to meet her as she left the floor.

''Dance with me,'' he whispered in her ear, his arms going around her.

Before she could protest, he looked over her shoulder, and what he saw made him change his mind. ''No. Dance with Pete.''

Chapter Five

Megan was primed to protest Chad's sexy invitation—
no, command—and his embrace, in spite of her racing
heart. Before she could do so, however, the flirtatious
cowboy had figuratively dumped her in his brother's
lap.

She stood gaping at him, unable to come up with a
single word. Every time he got near her, she couldn't
think.

"Dance with Pete!" Chad hissed under his breath,
and sidestepped her.

Somehow the intensity in his order, a sense of life or
death that couldn't possibly have anything to do with
a simple dance, impelled her forward.

"Pete, will you dance with me again? All these
strangers..." She let her voice trail off, sounding
overwhelmed, appealing to his gentlemanly side.

"You bet, Megan," Pete agreed, though he looked
puzzled.

Chad touched her shoulder briefly, as if in approval, and walked away. She released an exasperated

sigh even as Pete led her to the dance floor. Chad Randall was enough to drive a woman crazy.

She didn't want him to flirt with her, but he did anyway. Sometimes. And just when he was pressing her, ordering her to dance with him in a sexy whisper, enveloping her in his embrace, suddenly he rejected her.

As she went into Pete's arms, she looked over his shoulder to see Chad talking to a beautiful young woman. Dark like the Randalls, the lady was tall and fit, an outdoors woman with the stamp of Wyoming on her. And unhappy.

Megan was filled with unexpected jealousy. What was wrong with her? She'd rejected Chad every time. But she didn't want to, she finally admitted. She wanted to lose herself in his strong arms, feel his big body pressed against hers . . . all night long.

She was so intent on her thoughts that she missed Pete's lead and zigged when he zagged.

"Sorry," she said breathlessly, hoping he wouldn't notice her distraction.

"Probably my fault. I'm no Prince Charming," Pete said with a chuckle.

She leaned back to look at his strong, handsome face. "Don't be ridiculous, Pete Randall. All four of you would qualify as a prince in any woman's book."

His cheeks actually flushed, and he gave her a sheepish look. "Aw, come on, Megan. You know I'm not a ladies' man. That's all I meant."

Smiling, she only said, "You'll do." And he would. But not for her. For whatever reason, the man across the room, chatting up a local lady, was the only one who pushed all her buttons, including jealousy.

Chad had been joined by Jake, the two of them standing side by side, facing the young lady. Megan's eyebrows rose at the show of strength. Poor lady. If she'd upset one Randall, Megan suspected she'd have to fight all four of them. And that would be a formidable task.

While she watched, the woman pushed past the two brothers, and Megan noticed for the first time that she was accompanied by another man. Who was she? Ex-girlfriend of Chad's?

Pete swung Megan around, and she couldn't watch the unfolding events. "Pete, has Chad recently broken up with his girlfriend?"

This time Pete leaned back to look at her. "Chad? He hasn't been dating anyone in particular lately. He's kind of the love-'em-and-leave-'em type. Why?"

She should've known. "He seemed upset when a young lady entered the restaurant."

Pete lifted his head to scan the room. Megan knew the moment he found his brothers and the unknown woman. He came to an abrupt halt and the hand holding hers turned into a vise.

"Pete? Pete, are you all right?" Megan grew more concerned as she realized his cheeks actually paled.

He began dancing again, but without his fluid cowboy grace. It was as if he'd received a blow. Megan turned her head to see that the unknown lady had sat down at a table, joined by her escort, and the two Randall men were standing beside the table, still talking to her.

"Who is she?"

Pete, his teeth clenched, muttered, "Janie Dawson."

"Is she from around here?"

He nodded, his steely gaze never leaving the young woman.

Whatever she'd done, she'd upset the entire Randall clan. "Is she an old flame of Chad's?" she asked again, acid eating at her stomach.

"No!" With his sharp response, Pete swung her around so his back was to the young woman.

Finally the light dawned. It was Pete who had recently had his heart broken, according to Chad. Janie Dawson must be the culprit. "I'm sorry, Pete," she whispered. She truly felt sorry for him. She also felt dismayed—at the relief that filled her when she discovered the beautiful brunette wasn't Chad's old flame. How could she be so selfish to feel joy while Pete suffered?

"Nothing to be sorry for," he assured her in icy tones that made it all too apparent there was.

The music ended, and Pete led her back to the table, his gaze never straying to the other group. Before she could even sit down, another cowboy asked her to dance. Her declining response was broken off by a sudden scuffle across the room. It was loud but exceedingly brief. By the time she looked, the young lady's escort was on the floor, rubbing his chin. And Chad stood over him, glowering.

Even as she watched, Jake stopped Chad from continuing his brawl. Pete stood, and she quickly grabbed his arm. "Pete, stay here. Jake will take care of it." He didn't act as if he'd heard her, but he remained beside her.

Megan watched the other two brothers, her heart sinking. Chad must be more involved with the other lady than she'd thought.

When Jake and Chad joined them, Pete demanded harshly, "Is that the greenhorn from Chicago?"

Chad and Jake exchanged a glance, then Jake replied, "Yeah."

"Damn him," Pete muttered under his breath.

Megan laid her hand on his clenched fist in a comforting gesture. At her touch, he looked down at his hand and forced himself to relax his fingers, linking them with Megan's.

Relieved, Megan smiled at him and then encountered Chad's gaze. The fierce glint in his eyes was difficult to interpret.

What did he have to complain about? He'd been fighting over another woman. She lifted her chin and glared at him. He had no claim on her.

When Jake decided to call it a night a few minutes later, she breathed a sigh of relief.

TWO HOURS LATER, Megan wasn't feeling relief. After a silent drive home, everyone had gone to their rooms, grateful for the evening to be over. But Megan hadn't been able to forget any of it.

Not the immense attraction she felt for Chad Randall, nor the jealousy that had surged through her. What was she doing? There was no future in a relationship with him. His own brother had called him a love-'em-and-leave-'em type.

And she wasn't interested in putting her heart on the line anymore. Not for anyone. She just had to keep telling herself that.

After trying to read and seeing the image of Chad in place of the words, Megan finally tossed the book aside and shoved back the covers.

Maybe she could blame her restlessness on her muscles stiffening from the horseback riding she'd done that morning at the arena with Jake. It had been fun. But she'd spent the time wondering where Chad was. There was that forbidden subject again.

Snatching up her robe, she quickly wrapped herself in it and headed for the door. A glass of milk would cure everything.

The soft glow of a tiny light at the head of the stairs guided her down the hall. She tiptoed, hoping not to awaken anyone.

The stair third from the bottom creaked as she stepped on it. She'd have to remember that when she returned. It echoed through the house, magnified by her apprehension. Pausing, she waited for any response and was gratified when she heard nothing.

It was darker after she'd started down the hallway to the kitchen, but she saw a light under the kitchen door. Was Red still up?

Just as she got near the swinging door, the light under the door disappeared and the door itself swung open. For the third time, she bumped into Chad Randall.

Only this time was different. He was naked.

CHAD STOOD under the hot water, letting the steam build up around him. He'd hoped a shower might help him relax. He hadn't been this tense in a long time.

So far, it wasn't doing him a hell of a lot of good. Maybe because his head was filled with thoughts of Megan. He should've gone for a cold shower instead of a hot one. But in winter in Wyoming? Even he wasn't that much of a masochist.

With a sigh, he reached for the bottle of shampoo. By having his shower tonight, he wouldn't have to bother in the morning, which would give him an extra half hour of sleep. He'd need it at the rate he was going.

When nothing came out of the shampoo bottle, Chad stared at it and then shook it again. Damn! Nothing about this night was going right. First he'd had to watch his brother and Megan together, then he had to hold her in his arms and pretend it didn't affect him . . . and now this.

With another muttered expletive, he shut off the water and stepped from the shower. He eyed his jeans, but he didn't want to dress and undress again just to go downstairs to the storage closet. If the women hadn't been in the house, he would've just gone downstairs stark naked. Instead, he grabbed the towel off the rack and wrapped it around his body.

When he came out of the kitchen, carrying the bottle of shampoo, he was grateful for his forethought.

His arms went around Megan, and her body pressed against his was all that kept the slipping towel in place.

"Turn loose of me!" Megan protested.

"Uh, Megan, I can't," he whispered, holding her against him.

"Don't be ridiculous. Of course you can. This bumping into each other is getting to be silly."

"If I let you move, I'm going to be standing in front of you in all my glory," he returned, chuckling slightly. His glory was increasing all the time with Megan in his arms. When she stared at him, uncomprehending, he explained, "My towel will fall if you move."

He watched the movement of her throat as she swallowed, and longed to trace its slender grace with his lips.

"What—what are you doing down here in a towel?"

"Getting shampoo," he said, carefully lifting one hand from her back to show her the new bottle of shampoo.

"Oh."

"What are you doing down here?"

"I wanted a glass of milk."

She swallowed again, and he thought he'd die of hunger to touch her throat, to caress it, to nestle there against it.

"Having trouble sleeping?" he asked hoarsely.

"Yes. It was an exciting evening."

The way her gaze skittered from his told him she was referring to his brief fight.

"I couldn't help it."

"Help what?"

Her voice was cooler now, in contrast to her warm body.

"You know what. The fight."

"Where I come from, gentlemen don't settle their differences with fists."

He continued to hold her against him with the hand holding the shampoo bottle, but his free hand circled that throat and slid up to her jaw to lift her face to his. "Maybe where you come from, men aren't men," he growled.

"Don't be absurd! They certainly are."

"Then why did they let you escape?" he muttered, and did what he'd been waiting all evening to do. He kissed her.

Megan had been wondering what to do with her hands. From the moment Chad had pulled her against him, she'd tried to find an answer to that question. She couldn't rest them against his bare chest, as tempting as it was.

If she touched his skin, she knew she'd give herself away.

Once his lips covered hers, however, she had no choice. Her fingertips skimmed that warm, sculpted skin, covered with a trail of black hair. Like a blind woman reading braille, she learned the pattern of his muscular chest, tracing the curves, brushing across the pebblelike nipples, feathering against his strong neck and descending again.

Meanwhile, her lips were responding to his, opening to his urging, receiving his seeking tongue, her own responding. What this man could do to her in the space of seconds was incredible. This time, unlike yesterday in the snow, there was no soft approach, no brushing across her mouth. Chad went into high gear at once, and Megan couldn't keep from meeting him halfway.

She scarcely noticed when the shampoo bottle hit the floor with a thud. Vaguely she felt both of his hands urging her closer. Then one was undoing the belt that held her robe closed. She gasped when his warm hand slid inside and encircled one breast. With a moan, she folded both arms around his neck and pressed closer.

His lips left hers and joined his fingers as they pushed the buttons of her top through their holes. Then he passionately kissed each inch of skin as it was revealed.

Freed from his intoxicating lips, Megan's head began to clear. What was she doing? She shouldn't— As if he'd heard her thoughts, his lips returned to hers, to demand even more cooperation. They were magic, carrying her to another world, where all was perfect, loving and, of course, forever.

That word rattled around in her head until his lips departed again. Forever? *Love 'em and leave 'em,* Pete had said. Her eyes fluttered open just as he lifted her against him and used those lips on one breast, freed from the pajama top.

"Chad!" she gasped, not sure if she was protesting or urging him on.

He let her slide back down his body, a journey filled with incredible pleasures. "Megan," he whispered in her ear. "Let's go upstairs."

His words shook her. He was asking for more than a kiss. He was offering a night of mind-altering sensations, she knew. But morning would come.

It wasn't easy, but Megan shook her head no.

"Megan?" Chad whispered, and she heard the confusion in his voice.

She could understand his confusion. Her body wasn't too happy about it, either. But she couldn't face another heartbreak. "No. No, I can't."

Without worrying about his modesty, she pulled away and ran back down the hall and up the stairs as if she were being chased. And she was.

Temptation was on her heels all the way back to her room.

LIFE ON A RANCH began early. But if she hadn't planned a meeting with the other decorators, Megan wouldn't have appeared outside her bedroom before noon, since it was dawn before she'd gotten to sleep after the debacle in the hallway.

But she was a professional. She dragged herself from bed, her eyes almost as heavy as her heart, and headed for the shower.

Megan, Adele and Rita had their meeting, not necessarily a felicitous one, right after breakfast. When Rita left the table, Adele looked at Megan.

"This is going to be a huge project."

Megan nodded. "I know. It could drag out over several years."

"What would you think about a joint proposal, half by your firm, half by mine? I know your people do quality work, and I could work with you."

Surprised, Megan sat up straight, thinking about what Adele said. It might mean her company could benefit without her having to spend much time at the ranch. "You know, that might be a very wise plan." She continued to mull over the ramifications. Then she looked warily at Adele. "But we should include Rita, shouldn't we?"

"Not if I'm going to be a part of it. That woman is a pain."

Red, working at the sink behind them, almost cheered. "Good for you. I'd rather give up a new dishwasher than have that lady hanging around here."

Megan and Adele exchanged guilty looks. "You weren't supposed to hear that, Red," Adele said.

"I'll keep my trap shut," he promised. "How about some more coffee?"

"I'm floating already," Megan complained with a grin. "Besides, I'll need to talk to the head of our firm before I can promise to make a joint bid. I'll go call her now."

Half an hour later, Megan had her employer's approval. Megan was the only decorator available to work on the Randall project, and Geraldine agreed that it would be better to split the work, since there was so much to be done.

She returned to Adele, and they worked out a fair division of labor. Then Adele returned to the work area she'd confiscated in the living room.

Megan looked longingly out the kitchen window. The good weather had held, providing lots of sunshine, though the temperature remained around freezing. She'd love to spend some time outdoors.

"Go ahead, girl," Red prompted, as if he'd read her mind.

"What?" she asked, startled.

"Go for a walk or something. All work and no play, you know."

"I really shouldn't—" She stopped and grinned at Red. "All right, I will. And if anyone wants to know why I'm not working, I'll tell them I'm only following orders."

"Good enough," Red agreed.

Already dressed in jeans, a sweater and boots, Megan grabbed a coat and stepped outside, taking a deep breath of the crisp, cold air. It helped dispel her tiredness.

Then she began a brisk walk to one of the barns Chad had shown her two days ago. She wanted to visit Tinkerbell again. After spending a few minutes with the mare, Maybelle, making friends, Megan was thrilled when the filly allowed a brief pat on her little nose before dashing behind her mother.

Feeling more content than she had all morning, Megan left the barn, her gaze roaming the view. How could anyone be sad living here? Then she thought about the man who'd seldom left her thoughts. She couldn't be happy here unless— She dismissed such thoughts. Chad wasn't interested in anything more than a roll in the hay—or the bed, as the case might be.

She determinedly turned her thoughts to other things. Pete hadn't seemed happy last night. Unlike Chad, Pete wasn't a flirt. He'd said he wasn't a ladies' man and, by the normal definition of the term, he was right. But he was a man many a woman would've been glad to claim.

Yet Megan felt at ease with him, as if he were a brother. And she didn't want to see him suffer.

Her mind on Pete, she didn't notice a pickup truck coming down the long driveway. It hadn't quite reached the ranch house when the noise it made intruded on her thoughts. She watched, expecting it to stop by the front door. However, it veered to the left and headed toward the foreman's house she'd inspected with Chad.

The new vet.

Curiosity drew her in that direction.

As Megan reached the cottage, the truck drew to a stop and the driver's door opened. The tall brunette who emerged was a little older than Megan, probably somewhere around thirty, a striking beauty. Could she be the vet? Pete had explained earlier that a large-animal veterinarian had to be strong, and the woman didn't appear to be a weakling. But there was a soft, feminine air about her, even so.

"Hello?" Megan called out just as a little boy scooted out of the truck. She couldn't hold back a smile as he eagerly began looking around him.

"Hello," the brunette returned, smiling. "I hope I'm not too early."

"You're the new vet?" Megan asked even as she looked around for a man.

She walked over to Megan, extending her hand. "Yes, I'm B. J. Anderson. This is my son, Toby, and my aunt, Mildred Bates."

"I'm delighted to meet all of you. I'm Megan Chase, one of the decorators looking at the main house."

"That explains it. Pete said there were no women on the ranch," B.J. said. "Is he around?"

Megan looked out over the pastures and saw a couple of horsemen in the distance. "He and Chad had to move a herd early this morning. That may be them returning now. Can I help you with anything?"

"No. The moving van is supposed to be here this afternoon. We just thought we'd get a head start."

"Why don't you come over to the main house and have a cup of coffee? Red won't mind. He might even have some cookies, if anyone's hungry," Megan added, grinning at the little boy. He was adorable, holding on to his mother's leg and half hiding behind her.

B.J. smiled her thanks. "If you're sure no one would mind, I'd love a cup of coffee. Aunt Milly?"

"We don't want to be intruding," the older lady said with a frown. "Toby and I will go on in the house, if it's all right. I packed us a picnic lunch."

"I'm sure that will be fine." Megan turned to B.J. "Come on. I'll introduce you."

Red made the woman welcome. "Make yourself useful, Megan, and pour the lady a cup of coffee."

Noise on the back porch signaled someone's arrival, and Megan tensed. She hadn't seen Chad since last night.

"Red," Pete called before he appeared in the doorway, "have you seen—?" He broke off as he saw that the answer to his question was seated at the table. He strode across the room, his hand extended. "There you are, B.J. Your aunt said she thought you were here."

Chad came in after his brother, his hat in his hand, his sheepskin coat unbuttoned. His gaze met Megan's and then returned to the newcomer.

"I'm Chad, Pete's brother," he said, extending his hand to B.J. also.

Megan discovered her jealousy wasn't limited to old friends. She'd liked B.J., but she couldn't stand seeing Chad's admiring look for the newest arrival.

Before Megan could gain control of her emotions, they all heard more steps on the porch. She wasn't surprised to see Jake in the doorway, but she noticed Pete's concern and wondered what was wrong. She might be jealous of B.J., but that wouldn't be Jake's reaction.

"It's getting colder out there," Jake said, taking off his hat and hanging it up. He slipped out of his heavy coat, his back still to the company. "You get that herd shifted?"

Obviously he hadn't looked too closely at the group around the table.

"Uh, yeah," Pete assured him.

Jake swung around and started to the table before realizing there was a stranger in the group.

"Hello! The new vet must've arrived. I'm Jake Randall," he said to B.J., extending his hand.

She stood and met him halfway.

Jake, a warm smile of welcome on his face, said, "Your husband already at work?"

B.J. stared at Jake and then looked at Pete, uncertainty on her face. Megan searched desperately for a tactful way to break the news to Jake, but B.J., seemingly unaware of the tension, said, "I'm a widow."

With a dawning look of displeasure, Jake asked for confirmation of his thoughts. "Then who's the vet?"

"I am," B.J. assured him.

Jake stared at her, then turned to his brother and rapped out, "Pete, I want to see you in my office!"

Chapter Six

The kitchen was silent until Brett walked in. It seemed to Megan that everyone drew a relieved breath when he greeted them. Chad performed the introduction to B.J.

"Glad to meet you. Where's Jake?" Brett added, bringing back the tension.

"Uh, he needed to talk to Pete. Lunch about ready, Red?" Chad asked, turning his back on everyone else.

Megan fought a rising irritation. The man was ignoring her. Yes, he was absorbed with a situation right now, but other than that glance in her direction when he came in, he'd ignored her.

And that was what she wanted, of course, she reminded herself. But he'd wanted to take her to his bed last night. How could he so completely turn off the attraction they'd both felt? She certainly wasn't very good at it.

Even now she could imagine him shirtless, letting her run her fingers over him, pressing against him—

"Megan?"

She snapped to attention. "Yes, Red?"

"If'n you'd set the table, we'll be ready to eat in about five minutes."

Getting up, she sailed past Chad as if he didn't exist and opened the drawer that held the silverware. He immediately moved to the other side of the room.

She was vaguely aware of Brett chatting with B.J., but all her attention was centered on the contrary man across the room. When Jake and Pete reentered the kitchen, however, they held even Megan's attention.

Though Jake's voice was stiff, he nodded in B.J.'s direction. "Welcome to the ranch, Ms. Anderson. Will you join us for lunch?"

Megan couldn't help but admire B.J.'s calm. "No, thank you, Mr. Randall. My aunt is waiting for me at the house. I'm glad to have met all of you." With a nod, she strolled to the back door.

"I'll walk you back to the house," Pete hurriedly offered, and followed her out the door.

Megan returned to her chore of setting the table, but she heard Chad's comment.

"I gather that was a surprise."

"You could say that." Jake rubbed the back of his neck, his gaze still fixed on the door.

"Maybe the boy thought you wouldn't mind since there's other women around," Red said, and nodded toward Megan.

She found that remark curious. After all, she and the other decorators would only be here a few days. The veterinarian would be a permanent fixture. Jake's frown in Red's direction did nothing to clear her confusion.

"Are we ready to eat yet?" was his only comment, however.

"I reckon, soon as Pete gets back and the other ladies come down."

Having finished setting the table, Megan volunteered to call the other women to lunch. Red thanked her as he carried steaming platters to the table.

Pete was just coming in the back door when she, followed by Adele and Rita, returned to the kitchen. After a wary look at Jake, Pete took his place at the table, saying nothing.

Silence reigned for several minutes as dishes were passed around the table. Suddenly Jake raised his head.

"I almost forgot. While Pete and I were in the office, Mike Caine called. When he was flying over the area this morning, he came across a herd of cows up in the foothills. Not a large one, but maybe thirty, forty head. Who's available to send up there to check it out?"

Brett swallowed his food and said, "I can go if you need me, Jake, but I'm up to my eyeballs in tax stuff right now."

"Pete and Chad can go, I guess. I'd like a third rider, but the hands are working that new herd we bought in the east pasture. Okay?"

Chad nodded, though Megan noticed he didn't show any enthusiasm. Pete, too, agreed.

"I could go," Megan murmured, looking longingly at Jake.

"This would be a tough ride, Megan," Jake said, frowning at her.

"I know, but you saw me ride yesterday morning. I might be of some help to them. And I'd enjoy being back in the saddle again."

"It would be too hard, Megan," Chad protested, really looking at her for the first time.

So he thought he could tell her what to do when it suited him and ignore her the rest of the time? She had some news for him. "I'm tougher than I look."

"Why not come along?" Pete said, ignoring his brother's response. Turning to Jake, he added, "If this is a wild bunch, it might be easier to have a third rider."

"Do you mean it?" Megan asked, excitement bubbling in her smile. "I've even done some herding when I was younger. I'll do whatever you want."

"You're not going to finish your recommendations if you go off playing cowboy," Rita warned.

Megan looked at Adele. "I'll work evenings to get finished, Adele, I promise."

"I'm sure you'll manage," Adele responded calmly.

Megan, thinking about what she'd need to take with her—and, she had to admit, enjoying the consternation on Chad's face—paid no attention to the sudden silence that fell.

"Why would you need Adele's permission?" Rita demanded.

Megan exchanged a look with Adele before answering, "Adele and I are doing a joint proposal for Jake since it's such a big job."

"Why wasn't I included?" Rita demanded again, her voice rising.

It was Adele who again took the wind out of Rita's sails. "Because the job isn't big enough to be split three ways. Besides, you've indicated you wouldn't enjoy working with us." She continued with her meal, as if nothing was wrong.

Before Rita could complain again, Chad turned to Jake. "I don't think it's a good idea for Megan to go. It'll be an overnight trip probably. Could be dangerous."

"Overnight? I haven't been on a camp-out in years," Megan exclaimed.

"Megan, it'll be too cold. And you haven't ridden much."

"You're wrong," she said, staring at him. He was still trying to avoid her, was he? "I ride frequently at a stable near Denver. I just haven't herded cattle in years."

Jake ran a hand through his hair, looking distracted. "Are you sure, Megan?"

She nodded, grinning.

"Okay. Looks like I have a new ranch hand. Red, can you pack some supplies for them?" At Red's nod, he looked at Pete. "You'll need to leave right after lunch. Take a truck and trailer until you get to the trail up Tucker's Divide. The cattle were in a small valley a few miles away. You might find them by nightfall."

"Right. Put on your long johns, Megan," Pete advised. "You're in for a cold night."

"I don't have a sleeping bag."

"No problem. We've got plenty," Pete assured her.

Chad sat there and steamed. He didn't want Megan riding with them. He didn't want a threesome that would tear his insides out. He'd decided last night that his only recourse was to avoid her.

He tried to think of other reasons to leave her behind. Like her need for privacy. They'd have to pack two tents.

A sudden thought almost doubled him over. Suppose Pete and Megan decided to share one of the tents? Chad didn't think Pete and Megan were that friendly yet, but he knew that was what Jake intended. Even so, Pete wouldn't be that open about—about courting Megan. Would he? He was still too sore over Janie, wasn't he?

What if Megan offered you the chance to share her tent? What would you do? he asked himself. And knew his immediate answer. Cold, rocks, small space, none of it would stop him from making love to her.

Could he blame Pete if he did the same?

He shoved away from the table, unable to remain in the room with Megan and Pete. "I'm going to get my gear together."

"You've got time to finish lunch," Pete said, a puzzled look on his face.

At least Pete hadn't figured out what was wrong. And Chad hoped he never did.

MEGAN STEPPED into the shadowy barn, saddlebags thrown over her shoulders. Jake had given them to her to pack her necessities, though he'd warned she should take as little as possible.

"What's wrong with you, Chad?" Pete's irritated voice floated through the shadows.

"Nothing. But I don't think taking Megan is a good idea."

She stiffened in anger and almost called out to Chad to challenge him. But she thought better of it.

"An extra rider may come in handy. And we won't let her come to any harm. Pick out a good mount for her. Maybe Buck. He's reliable."

"Me? You—" He stopped abruptly and spun on his heel, stomping away from his brother.

Megan grew angrier. He clearly didn't want her along, though she didn't know why, since he was so good at ignoring her. But she wasn't going to let him keep her from going.

"Hello?" she called as if she'd just entered the barn.

Pete turned and walked toward her. "Megan! You made good time. We're almost ready. While I'm loading the other horses, why don't you mount Buck over there and see if he suits you? He's a pretty good cow pony."

As Pete was talking, Chad had brought over and unlooped the reins of a buckskin pony standing quietly with two other saddled horses and a pack mule.

"I'm easy to please. If you think he's okay, I'm sure he will be." She smiled sweetly at Pete, ignoring Chad.

After dropping her saddlebags by the door, she followed Chad and the horse out of the barn, into the cold air.

"Where's your hat?" Chad snapped.

She reached in her coat pocket and pulled out a wool cap, along with leather gloves. "I thought this might be warmer than a cowboy hat."

He grunted—she assumed because he could find nothing to complain about.

After pulling on the cap, she walked to the horse's head and introduced herself, scratching his forehead and giving him a chance to get used to her. Then she pulled on her gloves, took the reins from Chad and swung into the saddle. Again she patted the horse, talking to him all the while, before easing him into a walk. A minute later, she pushed him to a canter, circling the open area before bringing him to a stop in front of Chad.

"Well?" she asked, a challenge in her eyes.

"That was great," Pete called from by the trailer. "He suit you okay?"

"Oh, yes. He's as smooth as silk." She kept her gaze on Chad.

Instead of speaking to her, he crossed to his brother's side, and she watched as an animated discussion ensued. Pete won, as she expected him to, because Chad didn't have a leg to stand on. She was a good rider.

"Bring Buck over so we can get him loaded, too," Pete called after a brief word to his brother, smiling at her. "Then I think we're ready to be on our way."

Chad was scowling as she approached and dismounted, but she ignored him. Or tried to. Why couldn't she feel the same way about Chad as she did about Pete—brotherly?

Instead, the man sent her up in flames. She wasn't going to give in to the fire, of course. But she wouldn't mind tormenting him a little in the process. She wanted him to know he couldn't almost seduce her and then act as if she were a bag of cow feed.

"You pack a bag?" he growled.

"A bag? No, Jake gave me saddlebags," she said, stepping back inside the barn to pick up the leather pouches connected to fit over a horse's haunches.

"Hey, a lady who's a light packer. You're a rarity, Megan," Pete said, grinning.

She handed the item to Chad, who continued to look unhappy. In fact, Pete was the cheery one today. Chad had no reason to be upset. Ignoring the turmoil in her stomach, she decided to change the subject. "What did you think of B.J.?"

Like a Geiger counter, she registered very little response in Chad at the mention of the vet's name.

"She seemed okay."

"Will Jake be okay about her being a woman?"

Pete answered that question. "As long as she can do the job, Jake won't have a problem. He's just concerned that she's—she's too feminine." He grinned at Chad. "And beautiful."

"Jake noticed, huh?" Chad asked, for the first time sounding like himself.

"Yep," Pete replied. "It's hard to slip a beautiful woman by the Randalls." He grinned at Megan, then abruptly sobered. "Even if we don't know what to do with her afterward."

FOR A WHILE, the trail they were following was wide enough for two horses, and Chad let Megan and Pete ride together while he followed with the pack mule. The sight of Megan astride a horse shouldn't have disturbed him, but he found it sexy as hell.

All he could think about were long rides, the two of them together, then stopping and making love under a tree.

In the summertime, of course, he reminded himself as the cold wind whistled down his neck.

He was turning into a sick character, he decided, since whatever Megan did or said made him think of making love with her. He hadn't been this randy since his teenage days. He was going to have to start getting out more.

The sun was almost down when Pete stopped to make camp. They'd have to hurry. Once the sun disappeared in the mountains, it got dark in a hurry.

Pete instructed Megan to gather firewood while he and Chad put up the tents. Chad had to admit she did a good job clearing a space for the fire, even digging a hole with a sharp rock. Before they finished the tents, she had a fire going in front of them.

"You're a good camper, Megan," Pete praised as he turned around. "This tent is yours if you want to move your stuff in there. I'll get dinner started."

"I'll see to the horses," Chad mumbled, coming out of the other tent.

"Better get those two lanterns going, too," Pete called out.

Chad hauled their packs to the fireside so Pete could start cooking. Then he extracted the two kerosene lanterns, filled and lit them.

"Megan, you need a lantern in there?" Pete called.

Her head appeared in the opening of the tent. "No. I was just unrolling my sleeping bag. Want me to fix yours?"

"Sure," Pete agreed.

"No!" Chad snapped. The other two stared at him, and he felt his face grow red. "I mean, no need to put yourself out."

"No problem," Megan said mildly, staring at him.

He hadn't lost his mind. But he was going to find it hard enough to sleep tonight, knowing she was in the next tent. If he could smell her scent on his sleeping bag, he'd be in hell all night long.

Turning away, he tended to the horses, tying them to a nearby tree on a long rope. Then he set out some oats. There wasn't a lot of grazing in the winter up here.

By the time he returned to the fire, Pete had grilled some steaks and warmed up baked beans. Chad discovered Megan had made some quick biscuits for the Dutch oven.

"This little lady is handy around a camp fire," Pete said, smiling at Megan.

"She's handy everywhere," Chad declared, sarcasm heavy in his voice. He regretted his loss of control as Megan stared at him, hurt in her hazel eyes, and Pete gave him a piercing stare.

After that, Chad ate in silence, concentrating on his food, while the other two chatted quietly across the fire.

After they cleaned up their dishes, Pete stood. "I'd better take one of the lanterns and see if I can find some more wood. We'll get out of here faster in the morning that way."

"I'll help you," Chad said, jumping to his feet. He didn't want to be left at the camp fire alone with Megan.

"Nope. I'll manage. Megan might get nervous here by herself," Pete said. Without waiting for any argument, he disappeared into the darkness, only the lamp he carried making it possible to follow his progress.

The two remaining sat staring into the camp fire, saying nothing. Finally Megan shifted and then looked at Chad. "I'm sorry you're unhappy that I came along."

"What makes you think that?" he snapped.

He was surprised when a chuckle escaped her. "Really, Chad, I'm not an idiot."

"What do you mean?"

"You've been acting like a bear with a sore paw. You tried to convince Pete I shouldn't come. You even made an ugly remark about my biscuits. I make good biscuits!" she added.

"They're damn good. But I don't think you coming was a good idea. I'm sorry if I've been difficult, but this ride is going to be tough."

"Did I complain today?"

"No. But we had an easy ride up here. Herding cattle out of these mountains is going to take a lot more riding skills than today's ride. And it's going to take all day. We can't all ride back in the truck, you know. Someone's got to herd the cows."

"I did figure that out," she said dryly. "Don't worry. I won't slow you up. You might even find I can be helpful."

He didn't have anything to say about her helpfulness. Somehow, since he had trouble concentrating when she was around, he didn't think he'd consider her presence a benefit.

After several minutes of silence, she looked away from the fire. "Shouldn't Pete be coming back by now?"

"He can take care of himself. Don't worry about him."

He hadn't meant his words to sound so sharp, but Megan said nothing else, and he worried he'd insulted her again.

When she spoke next, he wished he had. He didn't want to answer her question.

"The lady last night. Was she the one who broke Pete's heart?"

Chad turned his head, searching for Pete. Finally, with no sign of his brother to keep him from answering, he nodded.

"Tell me about her."

"Why?"

"I was just curious. She's pretty, seems perfect for a rancher."

"What do you mean by that?" he growled. Janie was a friend of his. He wasn't going to stand for her being insulted.

Megan raised her eyebrows in surprise. "I just meant she seems the outdoor type. Doesn't she live on a ranch?"

"Yeah."

"Well, I thought Pete would want a wife who could share in ranch life."

"Of course he does. We all want that."

"You want a wife?" The skepticism in her voice bothered him.

"No! I mean, I haven't thought about it." And he didn't intend to, either, he assured himself. Pete and Brett might change their minds, but he and Jake would remain bachelors together. Where was Pete?

No sign of him.

"Well, you'd better think about it before you get caught by someone like Rita," Megan warned, arching one brow. "I can't see her living on a ranch."

Surprising laughter escaped him. "You've got a point there, but I can assure you Rita doesn't tempt me in the least."

"She's very pretty."

"If you like Barbie dolls."

"What do you like, then?"

He stared at her, wondering how she could ask such a question. "You have to ask?"

She turned bright red. "I meant for a wife," she returned sharply.

"I don't want a wife. I prefer staying single."

Her gaze turned stonier. "Then you'd better think before you act like you did last night. You might get trapped."

"I didn't—" he began, wanting to defend his behavior, but he didn't know exactly what to say. He couldn't say he regretted holding her, because he sure as hell didn't.

The sound of Pete moving through the woods halted their conversation, and Chad was glad. Megan had a knack for turning the most innocuous topics into something personal.

"Found plenty more wood," Pete called as he approached the camp fire. He dropped a load of branches nearby and came over to them. "Megan, if you need to, uh, you know, excuse yourself, there's a bunch of bushes right up the hill that will offer you some privacy."

"Thanks. May I take a lantern?"

"Sure." Both men watched as she made her way up the hill. When she disappeared behind the bushes, only the faint glimmer of her lantern through the greenery revealing her whereabouts, Pete spoke again. "Megan's a good companion."

"Yeah."

"You've been acting kinda funny ever since we started out. Is anything wrong?"

"Nope. Think we'll find the herd early tomorrow?" If not, they might be faced with another night camping out.

"I hope so. I promised B.J. I'd take her around and introduce her to people."

"Hope she works out," Chad muttered, his gaze fixed on the hill behind them. When the light began moving again, coming toward them, he released the breath he hadn't realized he was holding. What was wrong with him? She was perfectly safe twenty yards from the camp fire.

"You go next," he told his brother. "I'll build up the fire so it won't die out too soon."

Pete stood and took the light from Megan as she reached the camp fire. "Okay?"

"Sure. I'm fine."

"I'll be back in a minute. Chad'll be here, though."

Megan looked at Chad and then turned back to Pete. "I'm going to turn in. I'll see you in the morning."

Pete nodded and left the campsite. Megan looked at Chad. "Can I use the lantern a few minutes to get organized in my tent? Will you have enough light with the fire?"

"Sure. Keep the lantern with you. Pete will be back in a minute."

"Thanks." With a sweet smile that left him hungry, she turned and entered her tent.

Pete came back, and Chad left with the lantern. When he returned, Pete was already in the tent. He noticed the lantern was still lit in Megan's tent. She knew to extinguish it before she went to sleep, didn't she?

Just as he was about to approach the tent to warn her, he came to an abrupt stop. Her silhouette played against the side of the tent, a dark shadow against the light.

With several sensuous wiggles, she removed her jeans. Then she crossed her arms and grasped the sides of her sweater and pulled it over her head.

"Dear God, don't let her remove anything else," Chad moaned to himself, his gaze glued to the striptease she was innocently performing.

She leaned back and shook her head, running her fingers through her hair, and his hand unconsciously reached out as if to touch her. Then she collapsed on the bedroll and extinguished the lamp.

He wished he could as easily extinguish the desire that filled him.

Chapter Seven

Megan shifted in her sleeping bag, trying to find a soft spot on the hard earth. She'd done the same thing several times during the night.

"I'll take the horses to the stream for water," a quiet voice said, and Megan immediately recognized Chad's deep tones.

The sound of two pots clanging together indicated Pete was starting breakfast. Time to get up.

Even though her bed was hard, Megan had no complaints about warmth. She'd been snug in her long johns and sleeping bag. With reluctance, she unzipped the bag and scrambled out, hurriedly pulling on her jeans and sweater, then her boots.

"Megan, you up?" Pete called softly.

"Yeah," she answered, stepping through the tent door, running her fingers through her hair as she did so. She excused herself and went up the hill. When she came back to camp, Chad still hadn't returned. "Is it okay if I go down to the stream and wash my face?"

Pete grinned at her. "Sure, as long as you go upstream from the horses."

She grimaced. "I know that much, mister."

"Figured you did."

Walking down the hill, Megan marveled again at the easy camaraderie she shared with Pete. As she approached the stream, however, the other Randall, who tied her in knots, awaited her.

"Good morning," she said cheerfully, hoping to start off better than they had yesterday afternoon.

He turned to glare at her.

"Didn't you sleep well?" She noted shadows under his eyes.

"Not exactly," he said, snorting in disgust.

Confused, she stared at him. He acted as if his poor night was her fault. Did he intend to blame her for everything? "What are you talking about?"

Instead of answering, he shrugged his shoulders and turned his head away.

"Was I snoring?" she persisted. The man was driving her crazy. It only seemed fair to return the favor.

"Nope. Forget it, will you?" He turned his back on her again.

"Stop that!" she yelled in frustration.

He turned around, seemingly surprised. "Stop what?"

"Turning your back on me," she explained, finishing lamely. "I don't like it." And felt silly complaining about his behavior.

"What would you prefer? That I stare at you all the time? Tell you you're beautiful?"

The fierce gleam in his eye brought back their encounter in the hallway two nights ago. All her plans to avoid this sexy man would go up in flames if he came near her again.

"No! No, but I'd like us to—to act normal around each other."

His gaze roamed up and down her body, bringing a flush to her cheeks. He seemed to select and then discard several responses before muttering, "Yeah, right."

Without waiting for her response, he turned on his heel and led the horses back up the hill to camp.

Megan knelt by the stream and bathed her face in the frigid water, all the more shocking because of the heat that lingered in her cheeks.

When she returned to the fire, she clung to Pete's side, unwilling to be left alone with Chad again. It was too stressful.

Breakfast was over quickly. With the tents packed and the fire safely out, they mounted and headed up the trail. Again she rode with Pete, leaving Chad to bring up the rear with the pack mule.

"Do you think we'll find them?" she finally asked Pete.

"Maybe. Mike was able to give us pretty good directions. If they stay put, we should find them. Problem is cows don't usually stay put."

"Why are they up here? Isn't it too cold for them to be this high up?"

"Yep. We must've missed them when we moved the big herd down below for the winter. It's fortunate we've had an easy winter so far. Otherwise, they wouldn't be alive. Between the cold and the wolves, they couldn't survive."

"Wolves?" Megan asked in surprise.

Chad called from behind them. "Yeah, wolves. The government was concerned the wolves were dying out. They've reintroduced them to the state."

"But don't they kill calves?"

"Yeah. But they're a protected species," Pete told her. "There's nothing we can do about it."

An hour later, they had reached the top of the pass and started down the trail. Megan suddenly reined in her horse, causing Chad to stop just as abruptly.

"What are you doing, woman?" he roared.

"Listen!" She thought she'd heard the lonesome sound of a cow lowing. It came again, and she turned to grin at Chad. "Did you hear that?"

"Yeah. Looks like we've found our herd. Can you see them, Pete?"

"Not yet. But there's only one way to go." He continued down the trail.

About halfway down the mountain, Pete called a halt. "I think we're moving away from them. Seems to me the sound is coming from over there," he said, motioning to his left.

They all listened, then Chad agreed. "You're right." He looked around them in frustration. "There's no way to go left here. I saw an animal trail a little way back. Want me to go check it out?"

"We'll all go," Pete decided.

"It might lead nowhere," Chad warned. "Maybe you and Megan should wait here or go on. You might find another way in."

"No, I don't think we should split up."

With a shrug, Chad pulled his mount around, followed by the pack mule, and headed back up the trail. Megan followed in his wake, her gaze now fixed on his strong shoulders, making it difficult to concentrate on her riding.

"Pete," she said, over her shoulder, "I don't know much about cows, but—but they sound like they're in trouble." The constant lowing had grown louder as they had moved down the trail.

"Yeah." Pete didn't offer any explanations.

Chad came to a halt. "Here's the trail. It's not a big one."

Megan smiled slightly at his understatement. The trail was extremely narrow, just barely wide enough for one animal. She looked at Chad to find him watching her.

"Maybe Megan should wait here."

She stared at him, about to protest, when Pete spoke. "Why?"

"This trail could get tricky. And we don't know what we'll find."

"I don't want to stay behind," she said, turning to Pete, knowing he was her best hope to continue.

"You're not. Get going, Chad. We'll be right behind you." Pete's authoritative tones left no room for argument.

Megan held her breath while Chad stared at his brother. When he finally urged his horse down the animal trail, she breathed a sigh of relief.

For half an hour, they slowly descended, winding back and forth down the side of the mountain. Then Chad called a halt and pointed downward. "There they are."

With the last twist of the trail, a small canyon was revealed where the herd of cattle milled around.

"Why are they going in circles?" Megan asked, puzzled. "Why don't they leave?"

Chad moved his horse a little farther along the trail. "There's the reason. This is a box canyon, and there's been a slide of rocks and trees that fenced them in."

"Damn, they're half-starved! Look at them," Pete said, concern in his voice. He turned to Megan. "Cows aren't the most rational of animals at any time, Megan, but these are going to be a little crazy. Be careful."

"Do they have water?" she asked.

"Yeah," Chad said, pointing. "There's a stream. That's all that saved them." He urged his horse forward and completed the several more zigzags down the mountain. Megan followed, but she wondered what would happen now.

"Can we drive them up the mountain?" she asked Pete.

"Looks like it's our only choice."

When they reached the bottom, Pete ordered Megan to one side and he and Chad tried to drive the cows up the animal path. But the bottom of the path wasn't very clear, half-hidden by several bushes.

"We're going to have to lead them," Chad finally said.

"What does he mean?" Megan asked.

Ignoring her, Pete looked at Chad. "You or me?"

"Flip you for it," Chad said with a grin, reaching into his jeans pocket. He tossed a coin in the air, and Pete called heads.

"Tails. Looks like you get to lead the way, big brother."

"But if you won, why does Pete get to lead?" Megan asked, confused.

Pete grinned as he explained. "Leading isn't the fun part, Megan. The cow I'll rope is going to be mad as a hornet. She's going to resist or charge me. Either way, it won't be a picnic."

It sounded highly dangerous to Megan as she thought about the narrow trail leading up the mountain. "Be careful," she urged.

"Never mind," Chad said abruptly. "I'll lead."

"Wait a minute!" Pete roared. "You won fair and square. I'll lead. You and Megan get to push 'em up. And keep an eye on Megan."

"I'll be fine."

Neither man responded to her assertion. They were discussing the best cow to choose as the lead. Once they'd selected it, the two men cut the cow out of the herd, and Pete's rope sizzled through the air to settle around its horns. Rodeo cowboying at its best.

Pete set out for the mouth of the trail. When the cow resisted, Chad rode behind it, slapping its flanks with his coiled rope. The rest of the herd scattered, and Megan pulled Buck out of the way.

It was a struggle, but Pete finally got the cow on the path and started up the mountain. Realizing that they'd need to move quickly while the other cows could still see the leader, Megan began pushing the herd toward the path.

Chad turned around and discovered the animals already in place and looked at Megan in surprise.

"Out of the way, cowboy!" she called, a grin on her face. It felt good to show him she could be of assistance.

He circled the herd, joining her in the rear. She breathed a sigh of relief when first one and then others began the steep climb. Their only difficulty came when the animals, finally reaching something to eat, most of the small valley having been stripped, wanted to stop.

"Keep pushing them, Meggie," Chad called as he swung his coiled rope.

Meggie? She hadn't been called that name since she'd lived on the ranch with her stepfather Jim. Distracted, she almost fell from Buck's back when he darted off to chase a recalcitrant heifer.

"You okay?" Chad called, worry in his voice.

He *would* have to be watching the minute she slipped up, she thought in irritation. She waved at him to let him know she was fine and went after the stray.

When they finally convinced every last animal to save itself by climbing the trail, the horses were weary, as were the riders. Looking up the mountain, they could see Pete way above them, now leading the subdued cow.

"Whew! They were a stubborn lot," Chad complained. "You as tired as me?"

His question made it easy to admit her exhaustion. "Yes."

"Well, I hate to break it to you, but I think we'd better walk our horses part of the way up. Think you can make it?"

She swallowed hard and stared up the trail. Then, with a weary sigh, she slid from the saddle. "Yeah, sure."

Much to her surprise, Chad stepped closer and patted her shoulder. "You did a good job, Meggie. It would've taken me a lot longer working by myself."

She couldn't help beaming at him. His praise meant a lot. With a surge of energy, she smiled and thanked him and then led Buck to the trail. "Shall I go first?"

"I'd better go first. Can you lead the mule? Some of those cows might change their minds and try to come back down."

"What do we do if that happens?" she asked anxiously as she reached for the reins to the pack mule.

"Try like hell to get out of the way."

Fortunately none of the herd tried to return to the canyon. However, when they reached the main trail, Chad and Megan discovered some of the cows had started down the trail instead of following Pete up. Luckily, they were too interested in grazing to go far.

Mounting, the two of them rounded up the strays and pushed them up the mountain.

Megan's stomach grumbled, and she looked up at the sky to see if it was near noon. The sun was still visible, but unlike the day before, there were a lot of clouds moving in from the west.

"Chad, I think a storm may be coming."

He jerked his head up before looking at her. "Yeah. We'd better push a little harder. Once we get them down the other side, we can leave 'em if we need to, but we've only got about four hours before dark."

This time she checked her watch and discovered it was already after one o'clock. He was right. And they hadn't reached the top of the pass yet. At least the cows could climb two or three abreast now that they were on the main trail. That would speed up the process somewhat.

Four hours later, tired and sore, Megan could have cried in relief when she caught sight of the truck and trailer they'd left parked at the start of the trail. She hoped she could hang on long enough to reach it.

Pete was waiting for them, leaning against the pickup, his horse grazing nearby. "Glad you made it," he called as they rode up.

"That was a tough haul," Chad said.

Megan decided that was another understatement. She sat slumped in her saddle, not anxious to dismount because she was afraid she would embarrass herself by crumpling to the ground.

Chad swung out of the saddle and came at once to her side, surprising her. "Come on, Meggie. You need to get in the pickup and get warm. Go start the heater, Pete. She's worn-out."

Before Megan could actually move, Chad put an arm around her waist and pulled her down into his arms.

"M-my legs are shaking," she muttered against his chest.

"It's okay, Meggie. I'll carry you."

As he swung her up into his arms, she sagged in relief. "Sorry," she mumbled. "You must be tired, too."

"Just a little. And ready to eat one of those ornery cows. I don't like skipping lunch."

Megan thought she might be too tired to eat. When they reached the passenger side of the truck, Pete had the engine running and the door open.

"She okay?" he asked softly.

"Yeah. But she's exhausted."

"I didn't quit," she tried to insist in a strong voice. It irritated her that it came out a whisper.

Chad gave her a little squeeze before he released her. "You sure as hell didn't, Meggie. You can ride with me anytime."

She flashed her gaze to him, trying to determine his sincerity. "Do you mean it?"

"Yeah. I mean it." He touched her cheek with one finger and then backed away. "We'll see to the horses."

CHAD FELT GUILTY. He hadn't meant to respond to Megan quite so intimately. He looked over his shoulder to see if Pete had witnessed their little exchange, but his brother was already working on loading the tired horses.

He hurried over to help.

"How's Megan?"

"Okay. She was a gamer."

"Yeah. She was a lot of help. Aren't you glad she went with us now?"

Chad shrugged. "Think it's going to start snowing before we get back to the ranch?"

"Probably. I've been watching the clouds while I waited for you two. It had me worried."

"Yeah. I should stay with the herd, actually, and bring them in tomorrow," Chad offered reluctantly.

"You're as tired as me. They'll probably be all right. I don't think the snow will be heavy. Jake can send some of the men out to round them up."

Chad shook his head. "I think Jake will expect one of us to stay. And you should be the one to take Megan back.'' He must be crazy, he decided. But guilt made him insist that he stay.

Pete looked at him, maybe questioning his sanity. ''Are you sure?''

''Yeah.''

''I hate to leave you here, but I agree that Jake would want the herd brought in in the morning.'' Pete paused to think. ''Okay, you go get in the truck and get warm while I load the horses. Then we'll eat some supper before Megan and I head back.''

Chad didn't argue. He needed to thaw out before he crawled into a sleeping bag, or he'd be cold all night.

When he reached the truck, Megan was curled up in a tight little ball, sound asleep. He couldn't hold back a smile. He didn't know of a single woman, except maybe Janie, who could've made such a rigorous ride.

He slid onto the seat and gathered her against him. Only to make room for both him and Pete.

It wasn't long before Pete joined him. He took one look at Megan and said with a grin, ''Sleeping Beauty.''

Chad said nothing, staring at her.

''Think we should wake her up to eat or let her wait until I get her back to the ranch and she can enjoy Red's cooking?''

Chad didn't want to turn her loose. ''I think she'd prefer to wait.'' Without ever waking, as if she agreed with him, Megan snuggled against him, her head on his shoulder. He looked at Pete out of the corner of his eye to see if his and Megan's intimate positions bothered him, but Pete was opening the pack that carried their food.

"This is cold, but I need something in my stomach," Pete said, handing one of Megan's leftover biscuits to him.

"Me, too."

They added some lunch meat and shared a canteen of water. It wasn't gourmet food, but they were hungry.

"Has she stirred?" Pete suddenly asked, staring their way in the dark.

"Nope," Chad said softly, trying not to enjoy too much the feel of her against him, the warm breath that caressed his neck.

"Who would've thought a decorator from Denver could ride like Megan? She didn't complain once, did she?"

"Nope. Never even asked about lunch," Chad said.

"Well, I don't care if she wants to use Italian tile, I'm going to tell Jake to let her have the job."

"Her and Adele. They're working together now, remember?"

"That's right. Without Rita. I'm ready for that lady to be gone. When are they supposed to leave?"

"They came on Sunday, so I guess next weekend." It was Wednesday night, so Chad figured he had a couple more days of resisting the attraction he felt for Megan. Then he could forget about her.

Except when she came back to work on the house.

"Do decorators do a lot of the work themselves or send someone else?" he asked cautiously.

Pete chuckled. "I imagine we'll see a lot of Megan for the next few months. Maybe Jake will even offer to have her and Adele live here while they're working."

Chad felt as if the ground had given way beneath his feet. "I'm sure that won't be necessary. They probably send other people to do the work."

"Uh-huh."

Their talking must've disturbed Megan because she shifted in Chad's arms, turning so that her breast pressed into his chest. He swallowed and concentrated on not responding to her softness. A half hour of this torture, and he'd be ready for the funny farm.

They sat in silence until, out of the blue, Pete asked, "What did you say to Janie the other night?"

Chad chose his words carefully, hearing the tension in his brother's voice. "I suggested she and her friend find another restaurant."

"Not much to choose from around there but Cassie's Chili Bowl," Pete said, naming a greasy spoon with a bad reputation.

"That's what Janie said," Chad agreed with a wry smile.

"We didn't have any right to ask her to leave."

"That's also what Janie said." Chad added with a sigh, "Don't worry. I told her you weren't asking. I was."

"So why did you hit the greenhorn?"

Chad gave a laugh that held little humor. "He thought he could order me around. And his opinion of the Randalls wasn't particularly flattering."

"Hard to believe, isn't it?" Pete drawled sarcastically. "Probably matched Janie's."

More silence. Chad thought long and hard before he asked the next question, but he wanted to know the answer. He liked Janie. And she hadn't seemed any happier that night than Pete had. "What went wrong?"

He thought at first Pete wasn't going to answer. Or would tell him to mind his own business. Pete wasn't much for sharing his innermost thoughts.

Finally Pete said softly, "I wish the hell I knew. I figure it's the Randall luck. Like Jake. I shoulda known better, but she was so—so sweet. I thought—I thought wrong."

"But Pete—"

"Forget it, Chad. She made it clear she's through with me. It's no big deal," he said in a patent lie. "There's other women."

Chad instinctively tightened his hold on Megan as Pete glanced their way, and then he forced himself to relax. He already knew Pete and Megan had something going, particularly if Jake had any say in the matter. It wasn't a surprise. Hadn't he watched them hold hands after the fiasco with Janie and her escort? Keep their heads together the entire ride back to the ranch, as if they were sharing secrets? Hadn't Pete been the one to include Megan in their ride?

Yeah. He already knew Megan wasn't for him, even for a night. So it was no big surprise.

"Guess I better get us started back to the ranch," Pete said with a sigh. "I hate leaving you here."

"Don't worry about it."

Pete grinned at him. "I'll put up your tent for you while you roast your toes another five minutes."

"You don't need to do that, Pete," Chad protested.

But Pete was already getting out of the truck. "I'll be back in a minute." The door closed, leaving Chad alone with Megan.

He looked down at her face, pale in the shadowy darkness. Sleeping Beauty.

Hell, why not? he suddenly asked himself. She wouldn't remember, and Pete would never know.

His lips covered hers in a wake-up call.

Chapter Eight

Megan awakened slowly, stretching her legs beneath the cover, feeling content. Until her muscles protested. The pain brought back the events of the past day. And night.

That seemingly never-ending ride down the mountain in the increasingly cold air had been difficult. She'd been rewarded by Chad's tender care when he helped her from her horse. Then his holding her in the cab of the truck while Pete loaded the horses had been paradise.

The sweet kiss he'd pressed on her lips had awakened her, but before she could respond, he'd gently laid her against the seat and disappeared. In just minutes, Pete had slid behind the wheel of the truck, and they had driven back to the house. Without Chad.

How could a man ignore her one minute, rejecting her at every turn, and then treat her like something precious the next? He was driving her crazy. And why hadn't he come back with them? She supposed he'd stayed to take care of the herd, but it seemed to her the weather was worsening.

That thought had her shoving back the cover and going to the window. Big, fat flakes of snow were drifting down until the occasional gust of wind blended them into a blur. Fortunately the wind wasn't constant, but the thought of being out in the storm made Megan shiver.

And worry.

Had Chad come back? Was he all right? Would he be loving and caring as he was last night? Or would he revert to the cold and distant man who ignored her?

In the shower, with the hot water easing her strained muscles, Megan admitted that her attitude might be part of the problem with Chad. Her head told her to stay away from the man, but her heart leapt every time he came near her.

"Silly thing," she muttered to herself. Didn't her heart have any sense of self-preservation? The man had no interest in marriage—or anything else long-term. He wouldn't mind having sex, but he didn't want to make love. And she couldn't settle for anything less than love.

With a resolve to strengthen her resistance to sexy Chad Randall, she dressed in several layers of warm clothes and ventured out of the safe haven of her bedroom. Her defenses remained strong... until she reached the kitchen.

"Hi, Red, sorry I'm up so late," she said, greeting the man bent over a mixing bowl.

"No problem, young lady. I understand you earned your keep yesterday. You could've slept all day and not heard any complaints."

"I'll bet Chad and Pete didn't sleep late, though, and they worked a lot harder than me." She'd kind of hoped they'd be in the kitchen, figuring the snowstorm would keep them inside.

"No, probably not. Pete was certainly out early," Red agreed.

Her heart faltered a beat. "And Chad?"

"Haven't heard from him yet. He stayed with the herd, you know."

Concern washed away her feeble attempt to dismiss the man from her thoughts. "But it *is* almost noon, Red. Wouldn't he be back by now?"

Something in her voice must've caught Red's attention. He moved away from the counter and said gently, "Now, sugar, that depends."

"On what?"

"On whether he ran into trouble . . . or had something else to do before he comes in."

Her voice growing more strident in spite of her efforts to control it, she said, "What could he have to do in a snowstorm? Have you looked out the window?"

Red grinned. "Megan, this is Wyoming. It's winter. We always have snowstorms. It's no big deal."

In spite of her liking Red, Megan wanted to bonk him on the head. Fortunately for him, a buzzer going off on the oven took him out of her range.

"Go tell the other ladies lunch is ready," he said as if everything was normal.

"What about the men? Aren't they going to eat?"

"They know what time lunch is," he explained. "If they show up, they eat. If not, we have leftovers."

Red's easygoing attitude didn't soothe Megan's concerns, but she did as he asked and sought out the other two women. Rita was working in her room, and Adele had her work spread out at the dining-room table. Since their arrival, the women hadn't had a meal in the more formal room. Megan preferred the kitchen, but the dining room was elegant in its proportions.

"How was your cowboying yesterday?" Adele asked as she accompanied Megan to the kitchen.

"Wonderful...and exhausting. I'm glad I don't have to do it every day."

"Especially not in this weather," Adele added.

"Did you see Pete this morning?"

"Why, yes, I came down just before he went to the barn," Adele said. "Why?"

"Did he say anything about Chad getting back?"

"No. Didn't he come in with the two of you last night?"

"No, he stayed with the herd."

Adele shivered. "Rather him than me. I don't know how they stand conditions like today."

Since they'd reached the kitchen, Megan didn't bother responding to Adele's comment. Instead, she eagerly looked for any of the Randalls. "The men haven't come in?" she asked Red.

"Nope. They called from one of the barns. They're eating with the crew today. Said they didn't have time to clean up for lunch with you ladies."

"Is Chad with them?"

"Didn't say, Megan. Quit worryin' about the boy. He can take care of himself." Red's kindly glance brought a blush to her cheeks.

"Of course! I—I just wondered."

In Megan's opinion, lunch was deadly dull and the food tasteless, though she'd had no complaints about Red's cooking before. Perhaps the problem was that she could think of nothing but Chad's safe return.

After lunch Adele asked her to look over some ideas she'd had. Megan couldn't refuse since she hadn't worked on the decor for the past day and a half. But her heart wasn't in it.

After an hour's struggle, she left Adele and returned to her room.

"You've got to get control of yourself," she lectured as she stared out the window. "Chad means nothing to you."

Her heart whispered, *I'd feel the same if it was Pete.*

"Hah!"

Okay, okay, so she was lying. With a sigh, Megan gave in to her anxiety and swiftly changed her shoes for boots and gathered up a heavy coat, hat and gloves. She was going to the barns.

"Where you going, girl?" Red asked as she strode through the kitchen.

"I need some fresh air. Cabin fever." That was the best excuse she'd been able to come up with.

"You haven't been in the house even twenty-four hours yet. Cabin fever takes a little longer, I think," Red responded, a grin on his face.

"Maybe I have a new strain of cabin fever."

"I'll bet you do," Red agreed, grinning even more. "And I think its name is Chad."

Her cheeks flamed, and she couldn't meet his gaze. "Don't be silly, Red. I'm just going to the barns, that's all."

"Ah. Well, try the arena. I think that's where everyone is."

"Thanks, Red," she threw over her shoulder as she raced out into the snowstorm. Her heart was pumping with excitement, as if she knew she'd find Chad there.

She followed the path that led to the barns, but it had already been filled in with the falling snow. She estimated at least four inches had piled upon the old snow. The wind was stronger, too. She leaned into it as she struggled past the horse barn.

Once she reached the safe harbor of the arena, she slipped inside and leaned against the closed door to catch her breath. And then scan the arena for the one person she couldn't forget.

He wasn't there.

She rubbed her eyes, wondering if the wind had made her vision unclear. But no, she could pick out Pete along with B.J. They were both on the railing of a narrow chute at the other end of the arena. Thinking

Pete might have some news of Chad, she hurried over to him.

When she got closer, she realized B.J. was inoculating Pete's rodeo herd. Each bull was run into the chute, and B.J., perched on the railing, would lean over and jab a large syringe into the animal. B.J. must be stronger than she looked, since Megan realized it would take muscle to do this job.

She gingerly climbed a nearby rail. It wouldn't be a good idea to get close enough to be the victim of the angry patients. Timing her call to the exit of the latest bull so she wouldn't disturb the other two, she signaled Pete.

"Hey! How's our cowgirl?" he called out, a grin on his grimy face.

Since the cowboy nearby forced another bull into the chute, Megan had to wait to ask her question. She admired B.J.'s efficiency while she decided she preferred interior design to B.J.'s job, even if she did like ranch life.

"We'll be through here after two more," Pete called out to her, and Megan took his words as a signal to wait. She spent her time scanning the arena for any more Randalls.

When Pete, along with B.J., appeared beside her, she almost fell from the railing in surprise.

"Hi, Megan. How are you feeling after yesterday?" Pete asked.

"What happened yesterday?" B.J. asked.

"Megan went with us to find that missing herd. The ride down the mountain wasn't one I'd want to repeat any time soon. And she stood it like a trouper." He grinned up at Megan as if he were a proud papa.

"Thanks. What about Chad?" She'd intended to slide her question into the conversation, so it didn't stand out like a neon sign in the middle of the desert. So much for that idea.

"Chad? What do you mean?"

She couldn't believe Pete's response. Hadn't he even noticed his brother was missing? "Has Chad come back?"

"Haven't heard." He casually turned to look around the arena.

Megan could tell him his youngest brother wasn't in sight. In fact, he was the only Randall apparent to her eye. "Aren't you worried about him?"

Pete put his hands on his hips and stared up at her. "It will take awhile to get the herd back."

"Yes, but it's two o'clock, and the storm is growing worse. What if he gets lost?"

Pete rolled his head back and let out a roar of laughter. Megan jumped down from the railing, her hands clenched into fists. She'd thought the Randalls were loving, caring men. Well, she'd just changed her mind.

B.J. touched Pete on the arm. "I think Megan is really worried, Pete."

As if that had never occurred to him, he stopped his laughter and frowned at Megan. "Are you? Really worried?"

Megan could only nod.

"Honey, don't worry about Chad. The boy's part Indian. He could find his way back home no matter what kind of storm hit him."

"Maybe Jake, I mean, Mr. Randall, has had word of him," B.J. suggested.

Pete looked at her impatiently, "Call him 'Jake,' B.J. If you want to wait, Megan, I'll go ask him. He's on the phone over there in the office."

Again Megan nodded.

Once he'd walked away, B.J. slipped her arm around Megan's shoulders. "Men don't understand the art of worrying, Megan."

She couldn't hold back a sniff, but at least she didn't sob out loud. "I guess not."

"I haven't been outside in a few hours. How bad is the storm?"

"I guess not that terrible, but there's been about four or five inches that have fallen, and the wind is picking up." Megan kept her gaze on Pete's back, willing him to walk faster. When he stopped to chat with one of the cowboys, she actually groaned and then shot a look at B.J. "I tend to overreact."

"Then you'll make a great mother. Once you have a child, you spend half your life overreacting," B.J. assured her with a grin.

"Then it's a good thing that I don't intend to have children."

"Why not?"

"Because I'm not going to marry."

B.J. took her arm down and stepped in front of Megan so she could see her face. "I know men are weird, but what other choice do we have?"

Megan shrugged her shoulders, trying to sound nonchalant. "Some people aren't cut out for marriage."

"I've heard that line before, but it usually comes out of a man's mouth."

"Especially the Randalls." Megan said, making her own attempt at humor.

One of B.J.'s eyebrows went up. "Thanks for the warning. I won't set my cap for any of them."

Megan sighed. "Then you'll probably be in a crowd of one. I think every woman in Wyoming has them at the top of her most-eligible-bachelor list."

"I can see why. Handsome, charming, wealthy. Those qualities are always in high demand."

"Well, they'd better add mule-headed, hard-hearted, love 'em and leave 'em...." She trailed off when she saw Pete emerge from the office. "Here comes Pete."

"Hey, Doc!" a cowboy called from over by the chute.

"Will you be all right until Pete gets here?" B.J. asked.

Megan felt ashamed that her distress had been so obvious. "Of course I will. Go do your work. And B.J....thanks."

The vet smiled and got back to work.

Megan couldn't stand to wait for Pete to saunter back to her side. Couldn't the man walk faster than a snail? She headed in his direction, eating up twice the distance he did.

"Well?" she demanded breathlessly when she reached him.

"He's not back yet. But Jake sent a couple of our best guys out to meet him and give him a hand. They should be back any time."

She stared at him, incomprehension filling her. "That's it? You're not going to do anything?"

Pete seemed taken aback. "What did you want us to do, Megan?"

"You could go look for him yourself. I'd go but I don't know the area. I could come with you." She didn't realize how desperate she sounded until she saw the shock on Pete's face.

"Never mind," she gasped, and turned to run for the door to the arena.

"Megan, wait!" Pete called.

She guessed he could move fast when he wanted to because he caught her about halfway to the door. Unfortunately tears were streaming down her face. She'd shut her heart to so much that now that Chad had sneaked inside, the emotion was hard to control.

"Aw, Megan," Pete said with a groan when he saw her face. Without another word, he pulled her into his arms and laid his head on her hair. One large hand rubbed a big circle on her back, and he softly assured her of Chad's safety.

Feeling absolutely ridiculous, Megan brought her tears under control and wiped her eyes with the back of her hand. "You—you do that comfort thing awfully well." Her attempt to laugh didn't quite come off, but she tried.

"Thanks. Someone told me women like that sort of thing," he assured her with a wry grin. "You okay?"

"Yeah, sure. I'm not used to being out in the wilds, that's all. In the city, no one even gets in their car if there's a snowstorm, unless they have to, of course." She tried a smile this time and was more successful.

"Good for you." He leaned down and kissed her cheek. "If he's not here by dark, I can assure you Jake will have an all-out search going. We'll take the jeeps and bring him back. We Randalls take care of our own."

She nodded.

Before she could pull out of his arms, he gave her another hug. "Now, you go on back to the house so we don't have to worry about you."

"Thanks, Pete." She turned to follow his orders. But she couldn't quite bring herself to go back to the house. Instead, she stopped off in the horse barn. Somehow being there made her feel closer to Chad.

Mindful of her own worry, she called Red and told him where she was. Then she plopped down on a bale of hay next to one of the stalls and talked out her frustrations with the horses.

CHAD HAD SPENT a lousy morning. The herd, having found a little grass and shelter from the worst of the storm, wasn't interested in moving before daylight. It was well after sunup before he finally convinced them to move in the right direction.

By that time, he felt half-frozen, and the cold biscuit he'd had for breakfast didn't do much to fill his stomach. His mind played with the idea of a hot shower and a steaming bowl of Red's stew while his horse did most of the work.

About ten, when the two cowboys caught up with him, Chad was glad for the company. And even happier with the thermos of coffee and food they brought him.

"Thanks, guys. Did Pete and Megan get back okay last night?" He knew they must've, but he wanted to hear someone say so.

"Haven't seen Megan yet. Pete was down at the corral early. I think the new doc was going to start giving his bulls their shots."

"Good." Good, hell. The least she could've done was get up and show herself so he'd know she was all right.

"I think the storm's gettin' worse," one of the cowboys said. "We didn't think you'd have 'em this far along."

"It wasn't easy. They found a sheltered area and they weren't anxious to face the storm."

"Can't blame 'em. Let's push 'em a little faster now that there's three of us."

They made it back to the ranch a little after two, herding the cows into a large corral near the arena. The two cowboys hurried to the bunkhouse for a late lunch, offering for Chad to join them.

He refused, saying he'd check in with Jake and then call it a day. He intended to spend an hour or two in a hot, steaming shower, after he ate something.

Opening the door to the arena, where he figured everyone would be, he came to an abrupt halt. Not thirty feet away, Megan stood wrapped in Pete's arms.

It wasn't as if she was resisting or anything. She was cuddled right up against him. Chad watched as Pete leaned down and caressed her cheek. He almost doubled over from the pain in his gut. Without another word, he backed out of the arena.

Then he tried to decide what to do. He didn't want to go back to the house now. Megan could return at any moment. He couldn't face her now that he knew what he'd suspected was true.

Megan was for Pete.

All the indications had been there. But somewhere in the corner of his heart, Chad had been harboring the hope that he was wrong. That Pete didn't care anything about Megan. That she hadn't been claimed by one of his beloved brothers.

Because no matter what he felt for Megan—and he couldn't quite identify it yet—he wouldn't let her come between him and his brothers. Chloe, Jake's wife, had tried that. She'd even flirted with Pete. And look where it had gotten her.

He turned his footsteps in the direction of the bunkhouse. He'd borrow clothes from one of the guys and have his shower there. Then maybe he'd be able to scare up a game of poker or something. Anything to avoid Megan Chase.

She was definitely off-limits.

MEGAN SAT in the growing darkness of the horse barn, not bothering to turn on any of the lights. She was becoming quite chilled, but somehow she knew Chad would look in on his horses before he went to the house. And she was too anxious to assure herself of his safety to do anything else.

This compulsion she had was like a sickness. She'd already decided pursuing any kind of relationship with Chad Randall would be like playing Russian roulette. Except there'd be five bullets and one empty chamber.

Over and over she promised herself she just wanted to be sure he was safe. That was all. Once she knew he was safe, she'd go back to the house and try to avoid him.

The longer she waited, the more tense she became. With the snow falling, she couldn't hear any noise.

Surely she'd be able to hear an entire herd, wouldn't she?

When the door to the barn suddenly swung open and a light was flicked on, it took her a minute to be able to see who had arrived.

Then she leapt to her feet and charged down the barn. "Chad! You're safe!"

She wasn't sure what she expected, but it certainly wasn't for him to back away from her, one hand extended to keep her at a distance.

"Of course I am," he growled.

"But I've been— When did you get back?"

"A couple of hours ago." His voice still sounded wary.

"A couple of— What?" she almost screamed. "And you didn't let anyone know?" Suddenly she couldn't stand it any longer. With a bloodcurdling scream, she went for him, her fists flailing the air. She intended to make him pay for her suffering.

"What's wrong with you, woman?" Chad roared as he tried to avoid her fists. Then they both tumbled into a pile of hay, and Chad wrapped his arms around her to keep her from hitting him.

"What in hell is going on?" he demanded again.

"I've been sitting here worrying about you for hours! And you weren't even suffering!"

"So you're trying to beat me up? Women! You never make sense!"

The hated tears filled her eyes even as she struggled against him. The last thing she wanted to do was cry and appear weak. She ducked her head, but he lifted her chin.

"Aw, Megan," he muttered, and his lips covered hers as he pulled her more tightly against him.

Chapter Nine

Megan knew there was something she should remember. But wrapped in Chad's embrace, his warm lips loving hers, she couldn't think what it was.

Didn't want to think what should stop their kiss.

Suddenly he pulled away from her, a look of horror on his face. Feeling bereft, cold, she stared at him.

"I'm sorry!" Chad gasped, his expression changing to one of self-disgust.

"It was just a kiss," she lied.

"One that shouldn't have happened. My apologies. I'd appreciate it if you wouldn't tell Pete."

There was a sternness about his features that drove away the image of the flirt, the young man who chased women, according to his brothers. Megan was mesmerized by it and almost didn't hear his request. "Not tell Pete?"

"That's right. I'd appreciate it."

"No, I won't tell Pete...or anybody," she promised. "But—" she paused to swallow and try to remove her gaze from his lips "—it shouldn't happen again."

"No, not again."

They stood there, staring at each other in the gloom of the stables. Megan felt as if she were resisting the pull of a powerful magnet. Her head told her she wanted nothing to do with the handsome man across from her, but her body pleaded to move back to his embrace.

"I'll—I'll go to the house now. I have work to do," she finally said, and forced herself to move.

"Good idea," he agreed harshly.

Even then, she hesitated before walking away. Why did this man have so much hold over her? Her mother's experiences had taught her well to avoid all handsome, arrogant men, those who played women like instruments. She'd identified Chad as a member of that group when she'd first arrived.

Memories of the heartache her mother had suffered, *she* had suffered, strengthened her resolve, and Megan walked out of the barn. The sky was overcast, as if it still hadn't emptied its offerings, and the wind blew sharply. Coldness surrounded her inside and out.

She needed to get away from the Randalls. They were an attractive family. Not only was Chad a temptation, but his brothers were, too. To have a family, a loving family, had been one of her childhood dreams. Each time her mother married she'd thought, as a child, that she had a chance to become part of one. Each time she'd been proved wrong.

No, the Randalls reminded her too much of the disappointments and heartaches she'd suffered. If she added to that pain the danger in falling for Chad Randall, she knew she faced major devastation.

Determined to gird her heart against such weaknesses, she trudged sturdily toward the house. It was time to think about her job. That was her lifeline. She'd concentrate on work and put any thought of Chad Randall behind her.

DARKNESS HAD FALLEN as Chad crossed the area from the horse barn to the house. He'd driven himself relentlessly for over an hour after Megan had left him, cleaning stalls that didn't need it, putting out more hay. He didn't go to the house for dinner. He'd had a late lunch, he assured himself.

He wasn't hungry. He didn't want to see Megan again. He couldn't bear to face Pete.

He had no excuse for his behavior. He'd known Pete was interested in Megan. His brother had shown him over and over again. And he knew Pete needed someone like Megan right now.

There were plenty of other women around. He didn't have to try for his brother's woman, he reminded himself in disgust.

Tonight he'd flirt with Rita if it killed him.

And it just might.

He entered the house with his head down, concentrating on redeeming himself.

"There you are, boy. We were getting worried," Red said, surprising Chad.

"Worried? Why? I was working."

"I know, but the weather's gettin' worse. And it's dark."

"I'm fine."

"Want any dinner? I've got some left over."

Chad gave him a weary smile and nodded. Red had played the role of caretaker all Chad's life.

As he sat down, Pete and Jake entered the kitchen. He mumbled a greeting, not looking either of them in the eyes. He was too ashamed.

"Chad, everything okay?" Jake asked, puzzlement in his voice.

"Yeah, fine. I'm having a snack."

Red put a bowl of stew before him, and Chad had an excuse not to talk, even after his brothers joined him at the table. The other two discussed the worsening storm and the necessary chores for the next day.

When Rita entered the kitchen, Chad remembered his vow.

"We missed you at dinner," she cooed, batting her lashes at him.

"I missed you, too, sweetheart, but the horses demanded my attention." The word of endearment stuck in his throat, but he was determined to undo any damage he'd done. His gaze flickered to Pete, but quickly returned to Rita.

While he finished his stew, he engaged Rita in conversation, listening to her long anecdotes about her popularity or her business successes. Red, working at the kitchen cabinet, sent him several disbelieving stares as he encouraged the woman, but Chad ignored him.

When he carried his bowl over to the sink, Rita asked her inevitable question, "What are we going to do this evening?"

Chad wondered if the woman went out every night in Denver. She certainly gave that impression. Even in his younger days, he hadn't been that dedicated a partier. But tonight he was ready with an answer.

"How about playing some pool?"

"Pool? You have a pool table?" she asked eagerly. "I'd love that. I'm quite good."

"How about Megan and I take you on, then," Pete said, rising. "I'll go get her."

Chad almost groaned aloud. He didn't want Megan in the same room with him, much less playing pool.

"Maybe she's too tired," he suggested hurriedly.

"Won't hurt to ask. She's had an easy day today. We didn't drag her out in the storm." Before Chad could stop him, Pete went in search of the one person Chad wanted to avoid.

"You okay?" Jake asked.

Chad pasted a smile on his face. "Sure. Looking forward to beating Pete. Right, Rita?"

"Of course. I'm very good," she assured him again with supreme confidence.

He avoided his brother's and Red's faces and escorted his modest partner into the back room, where a large pool table dominated.

They were selecting their pool cues when Pete and Megan entered.

"I'm not very good, Pete," Megan was saying as they approached.

Pete's arm rested across Megan's shoulders, and Chad looked away. He didn't need a repeat of the earlier scene he'd witnessed in the barn. He wasn't a slow learner.

"Then let's play for money," Rita said, an avaricious smile on her carmined lips.

"Against the house rules, my dear," Pete drawled. "But we could play for something else, like doing the dishes or mucking out the stalls."

Rita stiffened. "I don't *muck*."

Chad knew his brother well. To prevent the fight he knew would erupt from Rita to Pete's next words, he inserted, "How about the losers serve the winners breakfast in bed?"

"Okay," Rita agreed. "I might even think about making their task easier by sharing your bed," she added, her invitation blatant.

Pete muttered, "I don't think that will be necessary."

Rita pouted, but Chad breathed a sigh of relief. He wanted to make up for kissing Megan, but he didn't want to get carried away with his guilt.

Pete helped Megan choose her instrument and selected one of his own. Chad racked the balls. "Shall we flip to see who breaks?" he asked his brother.

"Sure," Pete agreed.

"Or you could let me break, since I'm a lady," Rita said, batting her eyelashes at both brothers.

Pete shrugged. "Sure, why not."

Chad was disgusted with her ploy for an advantage. The Randalls played fair and square. He sent his brother a look of apology.

With the break, Rita knocked in the seven, a solid ball. When she tried her next shot, she missed. Visibly irritated, she stepped back from the table, a frown on her face.

"You go next, Megan," Pete said.

"I'm not sure which ball to aim for," Megan protested, looking worried.

Before he caught himself, Chad thought of smoothing away her frown, putting his arms around her, guiding her, soothing her. He turned away to rub chalk on his stick. Anything to take his mind from Megan.

"I think the best shot would be the thirteen." Pete explained how to sink it.

"I don't know—"

"Here, I'll show you." Pete stepped to Megan's side and put his arms around her to guide her cue.

Chad studied the shelves lined with books, trying to think of the last title he'd read. Anything to erase the image of Megan with Pete's arms around her.

"You can't do that, Pete. She has to do it on her own. This is a competition!"

Immediately his partner's protest irritated Chad, and he turned back to the others. "This is a friendly game, sweetheart," he said, using the endearment to soften his reprimand. "Of course he can help Megan."

He moved around the table, noting that Megan was again wearing tight jeans and a sweater. He shifted his position so he wouldn't have to watch her bend over the table. Pete, after a grin at his brother, pointed out the direction Megan's shot should take and then put his arms around her again to guide her cue.

"Fix your fingers like this," Pete showed her, forming a rest for the cue. Chad moved farther away as her scent surrounded him.

"I'm—I'm not sure this is a good idea," she whispered.

"What's the matter, Megan?" Rita asked. "Afraid you'll lose the bet?"

Megan responded by making her shot, then watching as the nine ball hit the thirteen, knocking it into the hole.

Megan spun around, excitement on her face. "We did it! We knocked it in!" She seemed totally surprised by her success.

Chad raised one eyebrow, a crooked smile on his face. "Why are you surprised? Didn't you know Pete's good?"

"Yes," she said, taking a deep breath, her gaze meeting Chad's and then looking away. "All you Randalls are good."

"Thanks, Megan," Pete said with a bow.

"It's still your turn, Megan," Rita urged, bitterness in her voice. "And I don't think you deserve any more help from your partner."

Chad gave the woman a cool stare. "Don't be a poor sport, Rita."

"No," Megan said. "Rita's right. Pete shouldn't be helping me. I'll manage on my own."

Rita's mood improved considerably when Megan missed her next shot. And improved even more when Chad hit three balls in a row before missing. Pete stepped to the table and began his first turn. His run lasted for five balls.

"I didn't think I was going to get another turn," Rita complained as Pete finally missed.

"I was hoping you wouldn't," Pete agreed with a rueful shake of his head. "I shouldn't have missed that one."

Rita sank two balls, drawing them even. When she missed the next one, she looked at Chad. "We've still got a chance if Megan doesn't get any help."

He gritted his teeth but said nothing. But he promised himself this was the last time he'd be on a team with Rita. His idea of flirting with her seemed more and more difficult.

"No need for anyone to help her. She'll do fine," Pete said mildly, but he sent his brother a smile of commiseration.

Megan lined up her shot under Pete's direction. Chad closed his eyes as she bent over the table right in front of him. He didn't need any more visual stimulation to feed his dreams.

Without opening his eyes, the plop of the ball as it went in the hole told Chad Megan had done a good job. Rita's growl also confirmed it.

"Now you have to sink the eight ball, Megan, and call what pocket it's going to. That will be a little tougher," Rita assured her, a hint of taunting in her voice.

Megan bent over the pool table again, and Chad found himself holding his breath, hoping for her success.

When the ball rolled into the designated pocket, Megan let out a whoop and spun around, her arms in the air. Pete and Chad joined in her celebration, as if she'd won a gold medal at the Olympics.

Rita glared at all of them.

Before Chad could say anything, she slammed her cue back in the rack on the wall and stomped out of the room.

"Looks like your partner is a poor loser," Pete said, smiling at Chad.

"Looks like it. Good shot, Megan. I'll be serving you both first thing tomorrow morning." The thought of seeing Megan still tucked in her bed, her cheeks flushed with sleep, filled him with such longing, he decided he'd better escape before anyone noticed his reaction.

He headed for the door.

"Come back, Chad. We'll play three-way," Pete suggested.

"I'd better not. I've got some work to do," he told him, looking over his shoulder but not turning around. He hurried down the hall and through the kitchen, not stopping until he was standing on the back porch in the cold night air.

"You hoping to get sick, boy?" Jake asked from the door.

He spun around in surprise. He hadn't seen Jake as he'd passed through the house.

"Just needed a breath of cold air."

"How'd the pool game go?"

"Pete and Megan won."

"Aha. So Rita wasn't as good as she thought?"

"Is she ever?" Chad growled.

"I thought maybe you were interested in her tonight after the things you said in the kitchen."

"Nope. Just being a good host."

"Good. I'd hate to see you get involved with her. She reminds me of Chloe in some ways."

"Then you shouldn't have been worried. You know how I feel about your ex-wife," Chad reminded him.

Jake rubbed his arms. "Come inside and have some coffee. It's too cold to stay out here."

Once they were seated at the table, coffee mugs before them, Jake said, "Megan's not like Chloe."

Chad took a sip of his coffee to give himself a little time. "No, she's not," he finally said.

"She and Pete seem to get along okay. He's happier now than he's been since—in a while."

"Yeah." Another swallow of coffee. "Too bad they leave Sunday morning."

"She'll be back. I'm not about to choose Rita to redo the house. So Megan and Adele will get the job."

Chad had known all along that Jake would choose them. It wasn't a surprise that Megan would be coming back to the ranch. But it was a strain on him just then. Later, after he'd had some time away from Megan, he'd be able to handle the prospect. But not now.

"I think I'll walk down to the horse barn and check on that mare. It's getting close to time." He stood and crossed to where his coat was hanging by the door.

"Need any company?"

"No, I'm fine. I'm a little worried about this mare since it's her first. That's all."

That wasn't all. He was worried about himself, too. He'd never wanted a woman as he wanted Megan. Every time she moved, she incited his arousal. When he got close to her, it took all his strength to keep his hands off her. She occupied his mind night and day.

And she was for Pete.

When he reached the barn, he hadn't resolved anything, but he had at least put some space between him and his problem.

He was hanging over the half gate of the stall when he heard the barn door open. Expecting Jake, a mother hen if there ever was one, he turned to discover his problem had followed him. But at least she hadn't come alone.

"Hi, Chad. Megan wanted to see the babies again. Hope you don't mind," Pete called out.

"Of course not," he replied, but he turned away from them, staring at the young mare.

Megan stopped to visit with Maybelle and Tinker-bell, but Pete came on down the barn to lean against the gate next to Chad.

"How's she doing?"

"Okay. But I don't think it'll be too much longer."

"The storm's getting worse. They always deliver at the most inconvenient times."

The phone by the front door of the barn rang.

Megan looked up. "I always forget you have such modern conveniences out here."

Pete, on his way to answer it, explained, "Jake had them installed a few years ago. Saves us some time."

As Pete answered the phone, Megan moved to Chad's side.

"You shouldn't have come here," he whispered harshly.

She looked at him in surprise. "Why?"

"You know why!"

"No, I don't. We agreed what happened earlier wouldn't happen again. I just wanted to look at the horses. Besides, Pete came with me."

"I know he came with you. That doesn't stop me from wanting to kiss you again," he growled.

Her cheeks flushed bright red, and she looked away.

"I'm beginning to think you're a tease!" he added, determined to drive her away.

She turned to stare at him in horror, her hazel eyes filled with hurt as tears pooled in them. "I—I wouldn't do that!" she exclaimed.

"I'm not so sure," he complained. "It would explain why you're down here now, after I left the two of you alone."

With a final reproachful stare, she turned and stalked toward the door of the barn. Pete, hanging up the phone, looked at her, puzzled.

"Where are you going, Megan?"

"Back to the house...where I belong!" she snapped, glaring once more at Chad.

Pete followed her to the door and watched from there as she crossed the open area to the house, but he didn't go after her. Much to Chad's regret, he turned and came back to him.

"What happened?"

Chad shrugged.

"What did you say to Megan?" Pete insisted.

Chad ground his teeth. Why did his brother assume *he* was the one to say something wrong? "Nothing. I was just surprised that the two of you came out here."

"Why? You know Megan loves horses. In fact, you two have that in common."

And they both loved Pete. They had that in common, too, Chad reminded himself.

"You didn't tell her not to visit the horses, did you?" Pete questioned.

"Of course not."

"Well, you must've said something to upset her. Megan's not like Rita. She doesn't get upset for no reason." Pete stood waiting, a stern look on his face, much like Jake's.

"I told her—I told her she was a tease," Chad finally confessed, feeling bad about his words. But he'd been desperate to put some distance between them.

"What?" Pete roared, shocked.

"Well, she is. She knows I— I'm sorry, Pete. I kissed her. I broke it off as soon as I remembered. I shouldn't have, but—"

"As soon as you remembered what?" Pete asked, frowning.

Chad snapped the stem of hay in his hands and threw it on the floor. "As soon as I remembered she's yours. It won't happen again!" He turned to walk away, ashamed that he'd betrayed his brother in such a way.

"What are you talking about? Megan's not *mine!*"

"I mean, I know you have feelings for her." Chad was getting a little put out by Pete's reaction. Chad was making a sacrifice for him, and he didn't even seem to appreciate it.

"Sure, as a friend. You think I'm romantically— Come on, Chad. You know about Janie."

"You and Janie are through."

"And you think it's that easy? That I can put Janie out of my heart, just like that?"

The pain on Pete's face made Chad uneasy. His brother was still hurting.

"Listen, little brother, don't hold back with Megan for my sake. But be careful. Games of the heart can really hurt." Pete slapped him on the shoulder and turned to walk out of the barn.

"What about in the arena this afternoon?" Chad called after him.

"What are you talking about?"

"She was in your arms. You kissed her."

Pete grinned at his brother. "Jealous? She was worried about *you*. I was just comforting her." Without waiting for a response, he left the barn.

Chad stared after him, his stomach, as well as his head, in turmoil.

Pete didn't want Megan.

A big smile broke across Chad's face.

He did.

At least for a while, he cautioned himself.

Right?

Chapter Ten

Megan woke before the alarm went off the next morning. Not surprising. She'd had a restless night. Her thoughts had centered around a certain difficult cowboy.

Today was Friday. One more day of avoiding him, and she'd be on a plane back to Denver. After his accusation last night, she didn't think she'd regret leaving, even though she'd come to love life on the Randall ranch. It made the thought of returning to Denver unattractive.

But it was for the best.

The alarm went off, and she reached out to turn it off just as someone knocked on her door. She sat up in bed and grabbed the silk wrapper that matched the thigh-high silk nightgown she wore. Hurriedly belting the robe, she opened the door.

"Breakfast is served, madam," Chad said, a smile on his lips.

He hadn't been smiling last night. She was still angry at him and shook her head. "No, thanks. I'll come down for breakfast."

Raising the tray a little higher, he said, "I've already got everything ready. And you won the bet, remember?"

She remembered. She'd won in spite of his partner's taunting. His friendliness with Rita hadn't made the evening fun for her at all. But it was a good reminder of his history with women. Love-'em-and-leave-'em Chad. She guessed he'd moved on from her to Rita.

"Why don't you take it to Rita? I'm sure she'd welcome you with open arms."

"Come on, Megan, let me serve you breakfast in bed. Rita didn't win the bet. She doesn't deserve to receive the prize."

"Fine, give it to me," she suddenly agreed, and opened the door wider to reach out for the tray.

"Nope. You have to get back in bed. That was the deal."

"Have you already served Pete his breakfast in bed?" she asked. She wanted to know, if he was going to insist she adhere to the bet.

"I would've, but he was up early. I poured him a cup of coffee," he added, a smile on his lips.

Those lips. She looked away, hoping she could forget how warm, how persuasive, those lips could be.

He nudged the door even wider. "Go on. Get in bed."

She finally did as he ordered, but as she pulled the covers around her, she asked, "Why aren't you still angry with me? Not that you had a valid reason, but last night you were angry."

Instead of answering, Chad set the tray on the end of the bed and reached for the extra pillow to slip behind Megan. She leaned forward to make room and then realized how close that put her to Chad. Her breathing speeded up, and she leaned back against the pillows.

"Thank you for breakfast. Don't let me keep you," she said, hoping the man would get out of her bedroom.

"Here's your hat, what's your hurry? Sounds like you're trying to get rid of me, Megan."

"I wouldn't want to be accused of being a tease again," she said, wishing she could've kept the bitterness from her voice, but she couldn't.

He picked up the tray and settled it across her lap, and she thought he would then leave, giving her a break from the tension she was feeling. Instead, he pulled a chair up to the side of the bed and sat down.

"What are you doing?" she asked.

"I thought you might like a little company."

He sounded the slightest bit uncertain, which made her more accepting of his presence than she should be. Not that he was easy to resist. His brown eyes were warm, his smile filled with charm. Tight jeans and a red plaid flannel shirt covered his physical attributes, and Megan's gaze traced his broad shoulders and narrow hips hungrily before she caught herself.

"No, thanks," she said, picking up the fork to take a bite of scrambled eggs.

"You're a hard woman, Megan Chase," Chad complained, but he was still smiling.

"And you haven't answered my question. Why aren't you still angry? Why are you— You're trying to repay me, aren't you? You're teasing me with your— You're trying to charm me."

He leaned closer, his lips only inches away. "I'm trying to say I'm sorry, sweetheart."

" 'Sweetheart'? Aren't you confusing me with Rita? I heard you call her that last night. Or do you call all women 'sweetheart'? Saves remembering their names?"

"Megan, you're being difficult."

Anger was building in Megan. The past few days, when Chad had tried to help his brothers and had helped her on the trail ride, she'd thought she'd misjudged him. He hadn't acted like a conceited man, thinking every woman was waiting for him to cock an eyebrow at her in invitation. But now that arrogant flirt she'd first met was back.

"How kind of you to inform me," she said in frozen tones.

"Megan, why are you getting upset?"

"Stop flirting with me!"

"You're not comparing me to your latest stepfather again, are you?" Chad demanded, all the charm leaving his face as he frowned.

"Why not? You're flirting, aren't you?"

"Yeah, but— Damn it, Megan, I'm attracted to you!"

"That's not what you said last night!" she retorted, irritated.

"You're wrong! I told you I wanted to kiss you. And I still do!"

He leaned across the tray, one hand catching her chin, and those wonderfully warm, seductive lips moved in on hers. But Megan wasn't a masochist. The man would kiss her, then accuse her of seducing him. Without thought to the results, she drew her knees up in protest and shoved against him.

The breakfast tray, including a full cup of coffee, emptied all over her. Fortunately, because of her stubbornness, the coffee had cooled off a little, but it was a messy way to warm up.

"Hey!" Chad yelled, trying to grab the tray and only making matters worse.

Megan's scream as the coffee hit her and then drained down her sides coincided with his protest. "Ooh! Yuck!" she added as she started scooping scrambled eggs off her chest.

"Damn it, Megan, why did you do that?" Chad demanded as he picked a biscuit off the floor.

"Why? Why?" she repeated, her voice rising. "Did it ever occur to you that I did it because I didn't want you to kiss me? Does that make any sense to your macho head?'' The other biscuit was in her hand, and she couldn't stop from throwing it at his head as hard as she could.

Red's biscuits were notoriously light and fluffy, so her missile didn't do any damage, but it did surprise Chad. His eyes widened. Before she could apologize, something she actually considered, he stuck his finger in the strawberry jam Red had put on the plate and drew a line across Megan's forehead.

''What do you think you're doing?'' she demanded.

''Retaliating,'' he assured her calmly.

''Retaliating? I'm the one sitting in a lake of coffee. How dare you!''

''If you are, it's your fault. You're the one who upset the tray.''

''Only because you were trying to kiss me!''

''Well, how could I know you were opposed to the idea? You didn't protest before.''

Because she guiltily knew he was right, she gave up on the argument. ''Get out! Just get out of my room.''

''Fine!'' he agreed huffily, and rose to stride to the door. About halfway there, he stopped and came back.

She stared at him warily, not sure what he intended doing now.

''Go get in the shower. I'll pick up the dishes and strip the bed.''

''What?'' she asked in surprise.

''I said, go get in the shower. I'll clean up this mess.''

Damn him. The moment she had dug up enough anger to resist him, he had to do something kind. "I can clean it up. Tell Red I'll bring down the dishes—"

"I said I'd do it. It's my fault."

She couldn't argue with him any longer. If she did, she'd end up in his arms. And then she'd be in real trouble. With a muttered "Thank you," she gathered some clothes and escaped to the bathroom. And prayed that he'd be gone before she came back.

DAMN! That scene hadn't played itself out as he'd planned. In Chad's mind, Megan had welcomed him with open arms and invited him to share her breakfast and her bed.

A little overly optimistic, maybe, but a nice fantasy.

A fantasy that hadn't even come close to reality.

He entered the kitchen, expecting his brothers to still be at the breakfast table, but only Red was in sight.

"Where is everyone?" he asked.

"The latest weather report came through. Looks like this storm is going to be a big one. Jake said for you to hightail it to the barn and saddle up. They're going to bring all the herds in as close as possible. It'll save time for feeding them."

Chad shoved aside his concerns about Megan and hurried out. He met Pete halfway across the yard. "Where are you heading?"

"I've got to call B.J. She's already at her office in town. If she doesn't start for the ranch now, she'll be snowed in. Or maybe I should say 'out.'"

"Glad you thought of her. She wouldn't know, not being from around here."

"Actually Jake thought of her. You take Megan her breakfast? How'd it go?"

Chad looked away. "Fine. Gotta hurry. Jake's waiting on me." He knew he didn't convince Pete, since he heard him laughing.

As soon as Jake saw him, he ordered him to string the ropes from the house to the barns. "And add one to the vet's house," he added.

They'd used the rope system for years. When the snow was blinding, whoever took care of the animals could reach the barn safely by holding on to the rope. There'd been a number of cases of men getting lost between their houses and barns and freezing to death. Judd, their father, hadn't been about to let that happen on the Randall ranch.

The storm was building in its fury. Already Chad couldn't see the mountains. As he attached the rope to the front porch of B.J.'s, the front door opened and Mildred stuck her head out.

"Is everything okay?" she asked.

"Yeah. We're connecting ropes to all the buildings. If you need to come to the main house, just hold on to the ropes and follow them. Is B.J. on her way home?"

"Yes."

With the cold, wet flakes hitting him in the face, he told her to let him know if she needed anything and hurried to the horse barn. He had to check on the mare due to foal before he saddled up.

Everything seemed okay at the barn, and he crossed to the next barn to join the others. He was surprised to discover Red saddling a pony also. "What are you doing here?"

"Helpin' out. I left Megan in charge of the kitchen," Red added with a grin. "She wanted to come, too, but I talked her out of it."

"Good. You must be powerfully persuasive, though, 'cause I can't seem to talk that lady into anything."

Red laughed. "Maybe you're askin' too much."

Maybe he was. But her heart seemed about as cold as the snow this morning. Though he couldn't say the same for her kisses. They could heat all of Wyoming.

As he mounted and headed out to the pastures, he wished he had some of that heat right now.

MEGAN WORKED HARD on the redecoration plans until noon. Then, mindful of Red's charge, she went to the kitchen to prepare soup and sandwiches for the three of them. The fury of the snowstorm drew her constantly to the window, but she couldn't see much of anything. How the cowboys were able to work in such conditions she didn't know.

She began a fresh pot of coffee. Whenever they came in, something hot would be their first need. Next she put on a huge pot of stew, knowing it would fit whatever time frame she needed. With the storm continuing to intensify, she couldn't believe they'd stay out much longer. She hoped not.

"They're not back yet?" Adele asked as she entered the kitchen after Megan had called to her and Rita.

"No. I'm getting worried."

"Yes. I don't think I've ever seen such an intense storm." Adele moved to the window to stare out at the whiteness when Rita entered.

She stared at the table. "Sandwiches? That's all?"

Megan shrugged. "I was working. And I made stew for later when the men return."

Rita sniffed but said nothing. The three women sat down, and Megan watched as Rita made a multilayered sandwich that Dagwood would've been proud of. When the men were present, she barely nibbled at whatever Red served.

"You must be hungry," Adele said, eyeing the sandwich, too.

Ignoring both of them, Rita bit into her creation and chewed, staring into space.

Adele and Megan chatted quietly as they ate, perfectly willing not to include Rita if that was what she wanted. A few minutes later, however, Rita deigned to speak to Megan.

"I suppose, with the storm, you didn't get breakfast in bed. Too bad."

Megan would have liked to ignore the catty remark, but Chad deserved his due. He had tried to fulfill the bet. "No, Chad brought me breakfast in bed."

Rita's eyes narrowed. "Oh? Well, I hope you enjoyed it. You didn't win fair and square, you know." When Megan said nothing, she added, "He would've preferred to bring breakfast to me. In fact, I'm sure he would've if it weren't for the storm.''

"Probably," Megan agreed pleasantly. She stood and carried her plate to the sink and rinsed it. Adele did the same, but Rita left everything on the table and walked out of the kitchen. With a roll of their eyes, the other two cleaned up after the prima donna without a word.

"Adele, I'm going to bundle up and go to the horse barn.''

"Are you sure? It looks pretty dangerous out there," Adele said.

"Red explained to me about the ropes. Someone has to check on Chad's mare. He can't since he's out bringing in the herds.''

"What will you do if something's wrong? Do you know that much about delivering baby horses?" Adele asked.

"No. But I have B.J.'s number. She was supposed to come back. If she's here, she can come." She paused, thinking about the possibilities. "If she's not, I'll just have to do the best I can. I saw one born once, on my stepfather's ranch." But Megan prayed she wasn't called on to play midwife to Chad's mare. She'd be frightened to death.

But something was prompting her to go to the barn. Even if Chad had upset her, too many times to mention, she didn't want anything to happen to his horses. She pulled on her coat, gloves, hat and even a muffler, wrapping her face so only her eyes were visible, and slipped out onto the porch.

Even with the porch roof absorbing some of the fury of the storm, she could barely see. She grabbed the rope hooked to one of the posts at the edge of the steps and moved out into the storm.

Now she knew what they meant when the weathermen said visibility was zero. She couldn't see as far as the end of her own nose. Her eyes were useless, and she snapped them shut and ducked her head.

The important thing, the lifesaving thought, was not to let go of the rope. Whatever else happened, her hands were both wrapped around that lifeline.

The horse barn was the second building. The relief that filled her when she slipped inside the shadowy barn was almost overwhelming. Her breathing was ragged, and she leaned against the closed door, relishing the muffled sounds and the relief from the pounding of the snow and wind.

Finally she pushed away from the door and began brushing the snow from her clothing. The welcoming nickers from the horses pleased her, making her feel a part of the ranch, as silly as that sounded even to her. Then she heard the sound of a horse in distress.

Flicking on the electric lights, she hurried to the last stall on the left, where the young mare was kept. The horse was lying down on the straw, clearly in trouble.

"Oh, no!" Megan moaned, and began digging in her pocket for B.J.'s number while she raced back to the other end of the barn to use the phone.

It didn't work.

Trying not to panic, Megan pulled back on her gloves. Red hadn't said anything about a rope from the last barn to B.J.'s house, but Megan prayed there was one. If not, she didn't know what she'd do.

Her return to the storm almost took her breath away. But she had more on her mind this time than the rope. An animal was suffering, and she was the only one to summon help.

Relief filled her when she found the taut rope after the next building. Following it as quickly as the storm would allow, she reached the front porch of the vet's house. Then she climbed the porch and pounded on the door.

Though it was only seconds, Megan thought she pounded for several minutes before the door swung open and she fell into their entry hall.

"Lands' sake! What's wrong, girl?" Mildred demanded as she helped her to her feet.

"Is B.J. here?" she panted.

"I'm here, Megan. What's wrong?" B.J. answered before her aunt could, moving from the back of the house.

"One of Chad's horses. She's delivering, and I think something's wrong. I could see part of the baby, but the mare was down, and—and—"

"I'll get my bag."

Megan liked the way B.J. didn't waste any time. Mildred held her coat for her, and though she warned her to be careful, she didn't slow her niece down.

In no time, the two women were outside, B.J. following Megan as they traversed the yard through the blinding snow, guided by the ropes. Megan could only hope B.J. was behind her, because she couldn't see her.

Once she stepped inside the horse barn, she turned anxiously to wait for B.J. She panicked when B.J. didn't immediately appear. Just when she was ready to retrace her steps, the other woman entered.

They were both gasping, but Megan led the way to the last stall.

"Go to her head and see if you can calm her down," B.J. ordered, and Megan circled the mare to kneel in the straw and stroke her.

"The baby's leg is caught. I've got to try to reverse the process a little. Hold her tight, Megan," B.J. ordered.

Megan caught the halter with one hand and continued to stroke the mare's neck and talk soothingly. "Is it going to live?"

"I don't know. We could lose both of them," B.J. gasped as she struggled to free the newborn.

Megan closed her eyes briefly and sent a silent prayer for the animals' survival. Chad might make her angry, but he didn't deserve such a tragedy.

B.J. had thrust off her coat and rolled up her sleeves before she began working on the animal. Now she gave a cry of satisfaction and withdrew her arm, bloody past the elbow, as the mare strained under Megan's hand.

In almost no time, B.J. was easing the birth sac from a tiny colt, helping it to lie down in the straw before she turned back to the mare.

Megan watched, thankful B.J. had been home. Without the storm, she would've been in town and not arrived in time. Of course, maybe Chad could've done the same job, but Megan was glad *she* hadn't had to try.

"Are they okay?" she asked, her voice barely above a whisper.

"Looks like it. The next couple of hours will tell. I'm going to give mama a shot, so keep hold of her head."

When that was accomplished, they let the mare rest a few moments and then B.J. came to her head to try to get her on her feet. It took several tries, but finally the mare was standing. Megan stayed with the animal, stroking her, congratulating her on her first baby, while B.J. steadied the colt on his trembling legs and guided him to his mother's milk.

Megan moved to B.J.'s side, and the two of them admired the product of their work. They didn't hear anyone approaching until Chad called out, "Is everything all right?"

He was just inside the door, looking more like a snowman than a cowboy, but he raced down the barn before either of the surprised women could answer.

Megan beamed at him when he came to a halt beside them. "Look, Chad. She had a colt, and everything's all right, thanks to B.J."

"And Megan. If she hadn't checked on them and come to get me, they'd both be dead."

Megan drew in her breath as Chad stared at her, suddenly fearing that he would kiss her in front of B.J. Instead, he grinned at her. "Well, Megan, looks like you've got another horse to name."

Chapter Eleven

"I think B.J. should have that honor," Megan said, dropping her gaze from Chad's.

"No way," B.J. protested. "If you hadn't come to check on the mare, she would've died, and the foal with her. You do the honors, Megan. And if you'll excuse me, I'm heading home. It's been a long day."

Before Megan could think of a reason to keep the vet with her, preventing a tête-à-tête with Chad, the woman had left the barn. Megan finally shrugged her shoulders.

"Okay. But I'd like to know the father's name this time."

"He's a champion named Black Demon," Chad said.

"And what's mama's name?" Megan asked, patting the mare on her forelock.

Chad's cheeks reddened. "Licorice."

Megan's lips twitched, but she kept her expression solemn. "Then I think he should be called Black Sugar."

"Black Sugar? Is that masculine?" Chad asked.

"Yes. Masculine things can be sweet," she assured him, her chin raised.

Chad laughed. "Black Sugar it is. You're good with names, Megan." He looked at her and then turned his gaze away. "Uh, I'd like to apologize for this morning."

He would, of course, bring up the one subject she'd like to avoid. "That's not necessary," she mumbled.

"Yes, it is. I shouldn't have forced myself on you. I washed the sheets myself so Red wouldn't know."

"Thanks," Megan returned, and anxiously tried to think of some way to change the subject. "How bad is this storm going to be? Are we going to be snowed in?"

Chad shrugged his shoulders. "Probably. It's pretty normal around here for winter."

Megan couldn't think of anything else to say. Retreat seemed the best option, and she moved toward the door to the stall. Chad apparently had the same idea, because he almost crashed into her.

He reached out to ward off the collision and then jerked his hands back. "Uh, we seem to have a past history of bumping into each other."

"Yes," Megan replied, her voice strained. All she could think about was how warm and seductive his touch was, how easily she was lost in his embrace.

"I guess we can learn from our mistakes. At least we missed each other this time." His lopsided grin made her want to trace his lips with her fingers, to change the half grin into one that took over his face.

"True. And we should never get close to each other with a breakfast tray," she added, trying to join in the spirit of his remarks.

"Especially one that has coffee on it," he said, his grin widening.

"Or strawberry jam."

"I don't know," he said, his gaze going to her forehead, "I find strawberry jam particularly seductive."

Megan sucked in her breath and held it. "We're supposed to avoid these situations, remember? Not encourage them."

"Oh, right."

The mare nudged Megan's arm, as if asking for attention, and she automatically rubbed her soft, velvety nose. "I guess we should go back to the house. You must be half-frozen." Anything to end their togetherness.

"Yeah, I guess so."

He elaborately swung open the stall door and gave Megan a wide berth to pass through. She took one last look at the horse and colt before she headed for the door.

But she couldn't help thinking that in a year or two, when none of the Randalls could remember her name, they'd know Tinkerbell and Black Sugar. She would have contributed to the Randall future in a small way. It left a bittersweet taste in her mouth.

"Don't be an idiot," she warned herself. The longing that filled her when she thought of the future was a weakness she had to root out. She'd made up her mind a long time ago that marriage wasn't for her. As if Chad had marriage in mind, she reminded herself.

"Did you say something?" Chad asked, catching up with her.

"No, nothing at all." After all, what was there to say?

"Well, brace yourself. The wind is awfully strong. We don't want any more falls, do we?"

She couldn't even respond to his teasing. Had she lost her sense of humor, as well as her heart? She gasped at the thought. She hadn't lost her heart. It may have suffered a little damage, but she hadn't lost it. Had she?

"If it's that bad out, how did you find your way back to the house?" Her question was a desperate attempt to distract her thoughts.

"It was hard. But we used compasses and fence lines. We didn't expect the visibility to get so bad so quickly, though. Jake wouldn't risk his men to save cattle."

While he was explaining, she pulled on her gloves and wrapped her muffler around her face again.

"Ready?" he asked, and she nodded. He opened the door and, with a hand on her back, guided her out the door.

Again she could see almost nothing in front of her. Hanging on to the rope for dear life, she inched her way toward the house. But she had to admit, Chad's presence behind her, even if she couldn't see him, was a comfort.

CHAD BREATHED a sigh of relief when they reached the back porch. His body was exhausted from straining against the strength of the storm. It was only early afternoon, but he felt as if he'd put in twelve hours of hard work.

He started brushing down Megan after they reached the porch, but she pushed him away and did her own dismissal of the snow covering her. She was an independent woman, he decided with a frozen smile.

Too independent. And hardheaded. After the morning debacle, he'd decided he'd better slow down in his pursuit of her. At least he'd won a smile or two from her in the barn. Maybe this evening, he could convince her he wasn't all bad.

"That's enough," he muttered, reaching for the door. "Come on inside and let's thaw out."

The minute the warm air hit them, Chad felt better. And the savory smell filling the room reminded him of how hungry he was.

"Wow. How did Red manage a stew? He was out with us most of the day."

"I cooked it while you were gone. Red left me in charge of the kitchen."

"Well, as the person in charge of the kitchen, would you allow me to have a bowl before I take a shower? I think I'd warm up faster from the inside out."

"Of course." She moved toward the stove.

"Hey, you don't have to serve me, Megan. I can serve myself. You want a bowl, too?"

Her eyebrows went up in surprise. "Yes, thank you."

"Why do you look so surprised?" he asked as he filled two bowls.

"I didn't know women's lib had made it to Wyoming."

He gave her a friendly grin. "We weren't raised with a woman hovering over us. Red raised us right. Everybody does his job and everybody shares."

He set the bowls down on the table, side by side, and pulled out a chair for Megan. Together they began eating, conversation falling a distant second to their hunger.

The steaming beef and vegetables, seasoned with thyme, immediately began to thaw out his insides. "Lady, you can cook one mean stew," he murmured, smiling.

"Thank you."

Before he could make any more comments to reestablish friendly relations with Megan, Rita strolled into the kitchen.

"Chad! I wondered where you were. I've been so bored without you around," she trilled, and took the chair on his other side.

"Uh, I thought you had work to do." He hoped she had something to do. Last night, when he'd had to avoid Megan, Rita had proved useful. But tonight he didn't want to avoid Megan. Though he wasn't sure he'd have a choice as he felt her stiffen next to him.

"I finished already. Megan's the one who has to make up time. Don't you, Megan?"

"I'm afraid so. And a shower to thaw out my toes might be a good idea, too. If you'll excuse me . . . ?"

Before he could protest her departure, Megan was out the door. Right behind her came Jake and Pete, with Red trailing after them. Though he greeted his brothers, his mind was still on Megan and how he was going to make any progress if she was holed up in her room.

"Chad!" Rita complained. "You're ignoring me!"

He expelled his breath and tried counting to ten before he looked at the woman. "It's been a long day, and I'm tired."

"But what are we going to do for entertainment this evening?"

Jake must've sensed that Chad was losing patience. He stepped in to answer Rita's question. "We're going to watch a movie this evening. We just received a new shipment a few days ago. I'm sure Chad will join us after he has his shower. Right, Chad?"

"Sure, Jake," he replied, and stood.

Adele entered the kitchen before he could leave. "You're all back? Nasty outside."

After general agreement to that comprehensive statement, Adele continued, "So how does this storm affect our travel plans?"

Rita hadn't realized the implications of the storm. She looked at Adele. "What do you mean?"

"We couldn't get you to the airport in this storm," Pete explained, "and it wouldn't do you any good if we did. Planes aren't going to take off in a blizzard."

"How long will the storm last?" Rita demanded, an uneasy expression on her face.

"We don't know," Jake said, "but at least a couple of days. We've had them go on for a lot longer."

Rita appeared upset by their responses, but she said nothing. Jake rose from the table and joined Chad as he walked to the door.

"I need to talk to you," he said quietly, nodding toward his office.

Chad wondered what his brother needed to talk to him about, but he didn't hesitate to follow him from the kitchen. After all, Jake was the boss.

"In spite of what you said, you seemed interested in Rita last night. At least she thinks so," Jake began, sitting on the edge of his desk.

"No, I—" Chad began. Then he remembered his behavior at the dinner table the evening before and flushed. "Well, maybe I seemed interested in her for a while, but, Jake—"

"Chad, you know how edgy everyone gets in a storm, trapped in the house like we are. Play along with Rita, just until they leave. Okay?" He stood, assuming Chad would go along with his suggestion.

"I can't do that," Chad protested.

Jake turned to stare at him in surprise. "Why not?"

"Because—because I'm interested in Megan." Chad watched Jake's eyebrows lower. He hadn't wanted to upset his brother, but he couldn't pretend to pursue Rita with Megan watching his every move.

"No, Chad, Megan is for Pete."

"No, she's not."

"They're getting along well. Pete isn't as upset as he was. I don't want you interfering. I'm planning on expanding our family with Megan." Jake stood with his hands on his hips, his jaw squared in determination.

Chad frowned in return. "What do you mean, 'expand our family'? You expected Pete to marry her?" His voice rose in surprise.

"Well, of course I did. Why do you think I invited a bunch of decorators here?"

Unexpected laughter bubbled up in Chad. "I don't know. To decorate?"

Jake grinned in return. "I guess it sounds crazy, put like that, doesn't it? Look, Chad, one of us has got to marry. We need descendents, someone to come after us. Dad's gone. It's time we began producing the next generation."

"I don't see you going out looking for a woman to have *your* children." The conversation had turned serious again.

"Of course not! I tried marriage. I guess I'm not cut out for it. But you and Brett and Pete, you'll be great at being daddies. And I'll be the best uncle your kids have ever seen." Jake stepped closer and clapped Chad on the shoulder.

"Whoa! Wait a minute here, Jake. Pete or Brett, maybe, but not me. I'm no more cut out to be a husband than you were.'' Just the thought made Chad's skin clammy.

"You're wrong. You'll make a fine husband.'' Jake paused and then looked more closely at Chad. "If you're not thinking marriage, then what do you have in mind for Megan? I didn't bring her up here for your entertainment, boy. If that's all you've got in mind, leave her for Pete.''

Frustrated, Chad snapped, "Pete doesn't want her!''

"How do you know?''

"Because I was leaving her for Pete, but he said he wasn't interested.''

"Damn!'' Jake ran a hand through his dark hair and blew out a big sigh. "Now what? How about Brett? Does he have any interest in her?''

"She's not a platter of meat to be passed around, Jake!'' Chad protested, his insides aching. He didn't like the way this conversation was progressing.

"I know that! But after all my trouble to match-make, I'd like some kind of result other than you getting laid.''

Chad's hands involuntarily clenched into fists, and for the first time since they were boys, he was filled with the urge to hit his hero. "Don't talk about Megan like—like she's a groupie at one of the bars!''

Jake studied him, waiting before saying quietly, "So tell me what you have in mind if you don't mean marriage. A friendship? Going to be pen pals?'' Then his voice hardened. "Or was sex what you had in mind, brother? A fling? An affair? And if that's what you're planning, then why is what I said so wrong?''

Chad's face flushed. "There's nothing wrong with two people enjoying each other.''

"I used to think that way. Now I'm not so sure.''

When Chad would've protested again, Jake raised his hand to silence him. "I'll talk to Pete. If he really isn't interested in Megan, then I'll back off. But you be sure the choice is mutual and that you're honest about your intentions.''

"Jake!'' Chad protested, hurt by his brother's warning.

Jake ignored him and stomped from the room, muttering, "Damn matchmaking! I can't do anything right when it comes to women!''

Chad stared at the door Jake closed behind him.

Matchmaking? Jake was matchmaking when he'd invited the decorators to come? The man was crazy! He didn't even meet the women first.

And what was he, Chad, going to do now?

He felt guilty thinking about bedding Megan when Jake had intended her to be Pete's bride, to carry on the Randall family.

Jake was right, too. Pete had seemed more cheerful with Megan around. Had he denied interest in Megan too soon? Was he really interested in her but just didn't know it yet?

Chad suddenly felt selfish.

Selfish and unsatisfied. Damn, he wanted Megan. Every time he got near her, he had to fight to keep his hands off her. She seemed to occupy more and more of his thoughts. But marriage wasn't anything he'd considered.

He thought about Jake's miserable marriage.

No, marriage wasn't for him, just as it wasn't for Jake. And maybe Megan wasn't for him, either. Jake was right. Just taking her to bed to satisfy his urges didn't seem too honorable.

Damn.

MEGAN STARED at the big-screen television as she nibbled on popcorn. Seated between Brett and Pete, she'd kept her eyes on the movie from the very beginning, trying to ignore the cozy twosome on the couch across from them. Chad had returned to the kitchen after his shower and immediately begun flirting with Rita.

Proving Megan right.

He was a flirt, a man who chased after the nearest woman, without any regard to people's feelings. Just like several of her mother's husbands. Just like the man she'd planned to marry, only she'd discovered his true nature before she'd walked down the aisle.

Just like all men.

Unfortunately they were watching a romance. Jake had been intrigued by the title, *While You Were Sleeping*. The film had come out a year or two ago, and Megan had seen it then. And cried.

Not because of the romance in the movie, though it was satisfying. No, she'd cried because the heroine was all alone in the world and was tempted to lie because she coveted the hero's family.

Megan knew just how she felt.

This past Christmas, she'd spent the day alone. Her mother and her young husband were in the south of France. Not that her mother had forgotten her. No, Megan had received a box a couple of days before Christmas with instructions not to open until December 25. But a bottle of perfume, even expensive French perfume, couldn't replace family.

She'd kept busy. It wasn't the first Christmas she had spent alone, and it wouldn't be the last, she was sure. She knew all the tricks. New Year's Eve, she'd had a party, inviting everyone she knew. And she'd had the Christmas holidays to get ready for it.

"Can you imagine someone living in a city that big?" Pete asked softly.

"But there's so much to do in Chicago," Rita assured him. "You'd never be bored."

Pete shrugged. "I'm never bored here on the ranch."

Megan smiled at him. No, she couldn't imagine any of the Randall brothers bored.

When the main character, Lucy, gave her speech about loving the hero's family, Megan nodded. Yes, that must explain what had been happening. She was attracted to Chad, of course. There was no doubt that they had some kind of weird chemistry any time they got close to each other.

But she'd also wanted his family, just like the character in the film. She'd wanted to be a part of their closeness. And she'd wanted to move back to the country. Those years on Jim's ranch had been the best of her life.

No wonder she'd thought she was falling for Chad Randall. He was handsome, sexy and intelligent. He had a wonderful family. And he lived on a ranch.

She couldn't have concocted a more potent attraction if she'd tried.

Time to wise up, Chase, she warned herself. *These things never work out. Better to understand that now and not break your heart. Look at him over there flirting with Rita. If that's the kind of action he's interested in, then you're better off without him.*

There. She'd gotten things worked out. Now she could forget about Chad Randall and get on with her job. She'd make her employer very happy if she and Adele won the job. She might even get a promotion out of it.

Yes, she was lucky to have this opportunity.

So why did she feel like the unluckiest person in the world?

Chapter Twelve

Chad scarcely noticed the movie. He was much more intent on Megan, sitting between Pete and Brett. Was she interested in Pete?

Rita, seated beside him, reminded him of a persistent fly at a picnic. No matter how many times you swatted it away, it kept coming back. Not that he took the opportunity to swat Rita, tempting as that might be. He'd tried to discourage her interest in him, though, with no success.

She kept hinting about the size of her bed, her loneliness, her needs. He was surprised she hadn't had cards printed for advertising.

Too bad they couldn't take her back to the steak house in Rawhide. She'd find some willing cowboys there, but she was striking out at the Randall ranch. Especially with him.

When the movie ended, they all returned to the kitchen. Red had promised them hot apple pie.

"I can't believe anyone could eat more after the huge dinner," Rita complained. "Though, of course, I didn't eat that much, but with my delicate appetite, it doesn't take much to fill me up." She looked pointedly at the two other women.

Chad grinned as Megan ignored the catty remark. Adele wasn't as generous. "Maybe it was that huge sandwich you ate at lunch that really filled you up."

Rita pouted, and Jake hurried to change the subject, asking everyone's opinion of the movie. Under the cover of the conversation, Chad murmured, "You won't offend Red if you'd rather go on up to bed. He'd understand."

Her eyes opened wide, and she leaned closer to him. "Are you going to have dessert?"

"Yeah. Apple pie is one of my favorites." Rats. Maybe he should've given up pie if it would mean Rita's departure. But she probably would've suggested they do something together. The lady was nothing if not determined.

She reached out a finger to stroke his arm. "Maybe—" she paused to wet her lips "—maybe I'll go on up to bed, have a bubble bath, prepare—" a significant flutter of her lashes filled the pause "—for bed."

"Good idea," he replied enthusiastically. "A bubble bath would be relaxing."

"And sensual," she whispered. "Will you come... tell me good-night?"

"If it's not too late," he said vaguely, vowing to himself to stay up all night if necessary.

"Oh, it won't be. I'll be waiting."

Yeah. That's what he was afraid of.

Rita stood. "I think I'll pass on the pie, Red, though I'm sure it's delicious. My figure, you know." Again she ran her hands up and down her body and stared at Chad.

Finally, with a general goodbye to everyone and a heated look at Chad, she left the kitchen. Everyone ate in silence until Brett finally said, "You must not have any calories in you, Chad. The lady almost swallowed you whole right here at the table."

Chad wadded up his paper napkin and aimed at Brett's head as everyone laughed. "Any time you want to entertain the lady, just let me know. I'm only doing it 'cause Jake asked me to." He couldn't keep his gaze from Megan's face as he made his explanation. There wasn't any reaction that he could tell.

"I know," Pete said with a sigh. "It's a tough job, but someone has to do it."

"I haven't seen you making an effort with the lovely but obvious Rita," Chad complained.

"Of course not. Megan's my job. And talk about a tough one! The lady constantly wants to be entertained, waited on, flirted with. She won't leave me alone for a minute."

Megan, sitting next to Pete, dug an elbow into his side and grinned at him. "Watch it, mister!"

Chad was jealous as hell.

"I'm afraid Rita is a little spoiled," Adele said. "We're here as professionals. None of us should need to be 'taken care of.'"

Jake responded, "You and Megan have certainly conducted yourselves professionally. And I don't mind telling you that I will probably hire your two firms to do the job, so I hope you like spending time here."

Adele expressed her pleasure, but Megan remained silent, and Chad watched as her fingers tightened on the coffee cup she was holding. What did that mean? Didn't she like it here? Her enthusiasm had seemed sincere.

"And with Megan around for a while, all our animals will have terrific names," Pete murmured, sending a teasing grin her way.

"That's true," she said, relaxing, "and I've been thinking about asking Jake if I could rename the rest of you. I think Pete's name should be Teaser, Brett is Joker, and Chad . . . Womanizer."

The other two protested loudly, but Chad said nothing. He already knew her opinion of him.

"Of course, you got Chad right," Pete added. "He's known for his reputation with the ladies."

Chad groaned under his breath. Leave it to his brothers to sink him completely.

Brett, as if more sensitive to Chad's mood, said, "I don't know. He's been hanging around the ranch the last few weekends. I thought he was losing his touch until Rita came into our lives."

"I told you I'm only entertaining her because Jake asked me to. Isn't that right, Jake?" He pleaded with his gaze for his oldest brother to back him up.

"That's right, Chad, and you're doing a damn fine job. In fact, the way the lady was heating up, I think you might consider easing off."

There was more laughter and comments before Jake stood. "Well, I'm ready to call it a night." He carried his plate and cup to the sink.

Among general agreement, Chad panicked. It was way too early for him to go up. If he didn't go to Rita's room, she'd come knocking on his door. "I'm not ready for bed yet. Won't anyone keep me company?"

Chad figured there must've been some desperation in his voice, because Pete started a refusal and then changed his mind. "Why not? I guess we can sleep in until seven or so in the morning."

"I'll have another piece of pie," Brett said, getting up to cut a second slice.

"I'm not sleepy because I slept late," Megan said, "but I think you all must be masochists after the day you've had."

"Well, I'm not a masochist," Jake said as he walked past them. "You kids have fun. And don't stay up too late. We'll have to do a few chores tomorrow."

Adele accompanied Jake as he left the kitchen. Red, having finished rinsing their dishes, turned to the others. "Do your own dishes when you finish. I'm turning in, too. These old bones aren't used to being back in the saddle all day." He paused by the table to put a hand on Megan's shoulder. "Thanks for helping out today."

She smiled at him. "I enjoyed it, what little I did."

After Red left, Pete said, "I hope you're happy about getting the job here. We haven't upset you with our teasing, have we?"

"No, of course not. It makes me feel part of the— the family." She flashed a bright smile that Chad thought was a little uptight. "I was just thinking of the complications all the traveling will cause."

Megan stood and began picking up the dishes, and the three men joined her.

"Were you thinking about a boyfriend?" Pete asked.

Megan looked at him, puzzled. "What are you talking about?"

Chad's interest intensified, and he waited for Pete to explain.

"When you were talking about complications, were you thinking about a boyfriend? Someone who would be unhappy that you were out of town, here with four incredibly handsome, sexy bachelors?" He grinned at his self-description.

Though Megan smiled back, she only said, "No."

They rinsed the dishes, and then Pete asked, "No boyfriend, or no, he wouldn't be jealous?"

Chad was glad Pete was asking the question he couldn't ask, until it occurred to him that Pete's insistence was proving his earlier speculation: that Pete was interested in Megan. He stuck his hands in his back jeans pockets and studied the floor.

"No boyfriend at the moment, Pete, though I would never let my personal life interfere with my job anyway."

"A career lady, huh?"

"Yes." Her answer was crisp and dismissing, as if she didn't want to answer any more personal questions.

Pete leaned against the counter, studying Megan. "Why isn't a beautiful lady like you married?"

Megan burst into laughter.

"What's so funny?" Chad asked.

"Look at you. Four eligible, handsome men, none of you married, and you want to know why *I'm* not married? You're probably all older than me. Why aren't *you* married?"

Chad held his silence, but Pete answered her. "Some of us aren't cut out for marriage."

"Oh, so all women are cut out for marriage, but not all men?" she returned.

"Well . . ." Pete paused.

"That's not true," Brett suddenly said, a frown on his face. "I think it's because there aren't too many women around here. We don't have that many opportunities to meet women."

"Then why don't you go where you *will* meet some women. Unless you're not interested in marriage."

"That's what Jake did," Pete muttered. "Didn't do him much good."

"Why did Jake end up getting a divorce?" Megan asked. "I know it's none of my business, but I'm curious."

"Because she was a…witch," Brett said with a grin. "At least that's what Chad named her—Chloe, Wicked Witch of the East."

"She made Jake's life miserable," Chad said in defense.

"I guess we Randalls aren't very good with women," Pete added, and Chad was reminded of Pete's failed romance.

"That's not true! I don't see why all of you aren't married. You're charming, handsome, kind. You must not be trying."

Pete tensed up. "I tried! It—it didn't work out."

Megan reached out to touch Pete on the arm. "I'm sorry, Pete. I didn't mean— She must be nuts to let a guy like you get away," she finished with a warm smile. "But why—?"

"Jake chose the wrong kind of woman," Pete said. "He met her while he was in Casper on business and married her before he knew much about her. She was beautiful, but she didn't fit in here on the ranch. She wanted Jake to move to Casper."

"Leave the ranch?" Megan demanded, horrified. "Surely she couldn't expect such a thing?"

"Yeah, she did. She said it was sick, all of us living here together."

Brett chuckled. "She even hinted we were...
strange," he said, pausing to wiggle his eyebrows at
Megan.

She giggled. "Not a perceptive woman, I'd say."

"No, and a lot like Rita. She thought the world
should revolve around her," Brett continued. "Because he worked long hours instead of entertaining her,
she told Jake he was too dull to ever make any woman
happy."

"He believed her?" Megan demanded incredulously. She surveyed the faces of the three men. "You
all believed her, didn't you?"

Megan listened as all three men disclaimed belief, but
the only one who sounded convinced was Brett. Shaking her head, she said, "I can't believe you let a woman
like that persuade you that you weren't suited for marriage."

"Hell, Megan, as far as I can tell, she was right!"
Pete exclaimed, sadness on his face.

"Why? Because you had a fight with your girlfriend? Everyone has fights, Pete."

"Why are you giving us advice?" Chad demanded.
"You said yourself you didn't intend to marry. What
makes you the next Dear Abby?"

"I choose not to marry, Chad, because I'm not interested. But the four of you are going around believing you're not suited to marriage."

Pete growled something in response, and Megan
shook her head. "Sorry. You're right. I have no busi-

ness giving you any advice. I'd better go to bed before I get myself in real trouble.''

The three brothers stood watching her in silence. When the door closed behind her, Chad muttered, ''Not the four of us,'' and then regretted his slip.

Pete's gaze whipped to him. ''What do you mean, not the four of us? Who doesn't think marriage isn't for the Randalls?''

''Nothing,'' Chad muttered, and started toward the door, hoping to escape without explaining.

Brett, more curious than upset, unlike Pete, demanded, ''Who, Chad?''

''Yeah, who?'' Pete asked. ''You must be talking about Brett here. He's the only one—''

''No. I'm talking about Jake. He thinks *he's* not suited to marriage, but he's planning on sending the rest of us down the aisle.''

''Yeah, right,'' Pete said with a cynical chuckle. ''How's he gonna do that?''

''Hire a decorator.''

His brothers stared at him in confusion before first Pete and then Brett's eyes widened in comprehension. ''No!'' they said in unison.

''What are you saying, Chad?'' Brett asked, as if wanting confirmation of his thoughts.

''He didn't,'' Pete protested, his stare fixed on his youngest brother also.

''He did. He told me.''

''Wait a minute,'' Brett protested. ''It doesn't make sense.''

"He hired decorators so that we'd meet some women."

"You mean he really isn't going to have any work done?" Pete asked, suddenly appalled.

"Yeah, he's going to have the work done. Jake wouldn't be dishonest. But he intended— He hoped that one of us would...that is, he wanted— Hell!" Chad finished in frustration.

"Adele's too old," Pete mused aloud, "and Rita's too much like Chloe. It's clear Jake doesn't like her. I guess that leaves Megan."

"But why is Jake so intent on us marrying?" Brett asked.

"He's worried about the next generation," Chad explained. "Apparently, since Dad died, he feels responsible for continuing the Randall name. He wants us to have children."

Brett's face showed panic. "Kids? I'm not ready to have kids. We've got a few good years left, don't we?"

Chad slapped his brother on the back. "Don't get your shorts all twisted in a knot. You're not first on the list."

Pete stared at him. "That leaves you and me, little brother." Then comprehension seemed to come to him. "That's why you thought—" He stopped in midsentence. "Well, I've had enough soul-searching for one night." Before anyone could say anything, he shoved away from the kitchen counter and strode for the door. Brett followed him.

Chad stood alone in the kitchen, wondering how he was going to avoid going upstairs. He was afraid if he didn't go to Rita's room, she'd come to his. And he didn't have a lock on his bedroom door.

He didn't have long to contemplate his problem, however, because Megan reentered the kitchen, anger on her face.

"Megan? Are you all right?" All thought of his conversation with his brothers disappeared as he focused on her.

"Apparently all right enough to be a sacrificial virgin for the Randall brothers!"

He wouldn't have been surprised to see flames come from her mouth, her words were so hot. And accurate.

"What—what do you mean?"

"Don't act innocent with me, Chad Randall! I came back down to ask Brett a question about the office. I overheard you tell your brothers that Jake only hired decorators so he could find wives for all of you."

"Now, Megan—" His soft tone didn't soothe her.

"Are you sure he's going to have any work done? Or was this whole thing just a scam?"

"Surely you've been around Jake long enough to know he wouldn't do such a thing. Of course he's going to have the work done. And there were no strings attached to the job. He just thought— He was hoping— We don't meet many women out here."

"That's a pretty lame excuse, Chad. You could go somewhere to meet women."

"Yeah, women like Rita."

She put her hands on her hips, still angry. "There are other women. Pete found one."

"Yeah. And all he got for his efforts is heartache."

"Oh, please!" Megan protested, and began pacing the floor. "Just because you stub your toe, you don't quit the game."

Chad couldn't help grinning, and Megan whirled around to see him. "What's so funny?"

"You sound like a coach. It's kind of surprising to hear something like that from a girl."

She rolled her eyes in exasperation. "This is a ridiculous situation. And now we're snowed in. How can I face Jake, knowing that he only hired us as potential brides?"

"Aw, Megan, you won't tell Jake I told you, will you?" He knew Jake would forgive him. After all, he hadn't really told Megan. But he'd told Pete and Brett.

Megan sized him up with her gaze. "You didn't tell me, technically. So I suppose I could keep quiet. But it means you owe me a favor."

"Anything." He suddenly remembered the dilemma he'd been facing when she entered the room. "Uh, Megan, I have another favor to ask." He unconsciously took a step toward her, not even aware of his movement until she backed away, a wary expression on her face.

"What favor?"

"I need protection." He tried to look helpless, but he didn't think Megan was buying that pose. Her expression grew skeptical.

"What kind of protection?"

"From Rita."

Megan made a production of looking around the kitchen. "I don't see her."

"No, she's waiting upstairs for me."

Megan rolled her eyes again. "I think you've gotten yourself into this particular jam, and you can get yourself out of it."

She turned to go, and Chad sprinted to the door to block her exit. When she saw him run, she hurried, too. They arrived at the door almost simultaneously.

"Not another collision!" she protested as he captured her shoulders.

"Nope, I won fair and square."

"What do you think you've won, Chad Randall?" she demanded, her chin raised in challenge.

Chad had to fight hard to resist the urge to kiss her, but he knew if he gave in to his wants, she'd leave him stranded, on his own.

"Okay, here's the deal. I beat you to the door, so now you either have to remain down here with me for a while, or let me share your bed...room," he hurriedly added as Megan's cheeks flamed.

Chapter Thirteen

"What did you say?"

Her full, pink lips opened in surprise, and he desperately wanted to close them with his. But this wasn't the time.

"I said you need to stay here with me or let me share your bedroom. Bedroom," he repeated, making sure he'd said it correctly this time.

"You're being ridiculous." She tried to unsettle him from his position, putting her hands on his chest.

His arms came around her. "No, I'm not. If I go up this early, Rita is going to expect me to come to her room."

She rolled her eyes in disgust. "Don't go. She'll catch on in an hour or two."

"Not Rita. She'll come to my room. And I don't have a lock on it." His temperature was rising from her nearness.

Laughing scornfully, she suggested, "So sleep with her."

"No, thank you."

"Why not? She wouldn't be your first, would she?"

"Look," he replied in frustration, "I know you don't have a very high opinion of my behavior with women, but I've never slept with a woman I didn't like or respect. And I'm not about to change now."

She dropped her gaze to his chest. "Rita's not that bad. She's a little pushy, but I heard she recently went through a bitter divorce. That does a lot of harm to a woman's ego."

Something in her voice got his attention. "Have you been married?"

Her gaze jerked up to his and then away again. "No! I—was engaged once, but I didn't marry."

"Why not?"

"This conversation isn't about me," she protested, and tried to step back out of his arms.

He held her fast. "Why didn't you get married?" He wasn't sure why he persisted with his question. He figured he already knew the answer. When she stubbornly said nothing, he prompted, "He was a flirt, right?"

At that, her gaze lifted to his, her eyes as icy cold as the world outside. "A flirt? He was a lot more than that. He had several women on the side. And believe me, he didn't care if he liked or respected them. And he also didn't understand why his infidelity would upset me!"

Without thinking, he hugged her close against him. "He was an idiot."

She pushed away from him, and this time he let her go. "I'm not letting you in my bedroom, Chad."

"Then stay down here with me a while longer."

"I don't want to play any pool. I'm not good at it."

"How about a computer game?"

She stared at him with exasperation written all over her face, and he tried to look innocent and vulnerable.

"This situation is all your fault," she said in disgust.

"Yes, ma'am."

"I should ignore you."

"Yes, ma'am."

"I won't play computer games with you. But I'll watch *National Velvet*."

He let out a whoop that had her shushing him, then he picked her up and spun around.

"Chad! You're going to have Jake down here fussing at us," she warned, "or maybe Rita."

He set her back down on the floor. "I'll be as quiet as a mouse." Then he took her hand and headed down the hall to the TV room.

SOME NOISE WAS DISTURBING his sleep. Chad shifted slightly, only to find his movement constrained by something heavy on his chest. His eyes slowly opened to stare down at Megan's sweet face, her warm body sprawled across his.

He was in heaven.

No, he was in the TV room.

Ah, last night. He remembered now. They'd started watching the movie, sitting circumspectly apart. Then, as the night grew chillier, he'd pulled out a blanket to cover both of them. They'd taken off their shoes and gotten comfortable on the extrawide sofa and the hassock in front of it.

Now Megan was stretched out the length of the sofa, her head on his chest, while his legs were propped on the hassock. He felt a distinct stiffness in his neck, but he wasn't going to complain.

Even as he wondered what time it was, considering trying to ease his arm from under Megan to look at his watch, the door to the TV room was thrown open.

"Aha!" Rita shouted.

Chad turned his head to warn her not to wake Megan and discovered she wasn't alone. Almost every other member of the household was right behind her.

"What's going on?" Jake asked, stepping past Rita. "Are you two okay?"

Megan's eyes fluttered open, and Chad grinned at her. A slow, dreamy smile spread across her lips, and he wished they were alone.

"Megan? Is everything all right?" Adele asked.

Awareness shot into Megan's gaze, and she bolted upright. "What?"

"We fell asleep watching a movie last night," Chad hurriedly explained to their audience. "That's all. What's wrong with everyone?"

"I couldn't find you," Rita said angrily. "I thought you were going to come...tell me good-night." She looked around self-consciously at her last statement, but Chad wasn't buying the act. The lady knew exactly what she was saying.

"No. I was busy." He didn't want to be cruel, but he was tired of, as Megan put it, playing that game, even for the sake of peace.

"Sorry we woke you," Jake said. "When Rita didn't find Megan in her bedroom or downstairs, she asked about you. Brett checked your room. With both of you missing, I thought we should search the house before we went out to the barns."

"Is the storm still raging?" Chad asked, unable to see out with the drapes closed.

"Yeah…inside and out," Brett said with a chuckle.

Rita sent him a killer look and stomped out of the room.

"Um, Red wants to know if you want breakfast. Everyone else has eaten," Jake asked, ignoring Rita's behavior.

"Yeah, sure. Give us a minute to wake up," Chad asked, already feeling the loss as Megan sat beside him now, her cheeks red.

As Jake shooed everyone out of the room and closed the door softly behind him, Chad sagged against the cushions in relief. "Sorry, Megan. I didn't mean to cause a scene."

"It's not your fault. I'm as guilty as you."

He noticed she didn't look at him. "Hell, we're not guilty of anything but being tired. Jake's not upset. The only one who cares is Rita. It's no big deal."

She gave him an awkward smile and stood. "Do you think I have time for a quick shower before breakfast? I feel . . . disheveled."

"Sure. But on you, disheveled looks good." And had felt good, too. In fact, her warm, flushed body pressed against his had felt sensational.

Blushing, she turned to the door. There, she paused to say, "I enjoyed watching the movie with you." Then she was gone.

He breathed out a deep sigh of frustration and longing. Enjoyed it? Oh, yeah. He only wished he hadn't fallen asleep. Then he could remember holding her. As it was, he only had those couple of minutes this morning.

MEGAN STEPPED OUT of the shower, dried off and wrapped the towel around her before opening the door to her bedroom. She came to an abrupt halt when she discovered a visitor.

"Hello, Rita. Did you want something?"

"Yes! I want Chad." The woman's face was tight with anger, and her arms were crossed over her chest.

"Then you need to talk to Chad, not me. He's not mine to give away."

"Not yet, but I'll have to give you credit for trying."

"I'd like you to leave so I can dress. Red is waiting to fix breakfast for me."

"That old man would fix you breakfast at midnight if you wanted it. You've certainly done your best to get in good with everyone around here. You think that will get you the contract, don't you?"

Megan chewed her bottom lip while she tried to decide on a response that would bring this conversation to an end. Finally she said, "Rita, I realize you're angry, but I have no interest in discussing any of this with you. Please leave."

"Keep your hands off Chad!"

"As I said before, you need to discuss your relationship with Chad, not me." She moved to the dresser and pulled out her clothes, trying to ignore the other woman.

"You were just playing hard-to-get, weren't you?" Rita demanded, following her.

"What are you talking about?"

"When we first arrived, you acted like you weren't interested in him, to draw his attention."

Wordlessly Megan gathered her clothing and went back to the bathroom, with Rita dogging her heels like a pit bull. The only way to get rid of Rita was to shut the door in her face.

"I'm not going to give up!" Rita screamed through the door, pounding it with her fist. "I want Chad!"

Megan dressed calmly, ignoring the muffled sounds coming through the door.

Why wasn't she more upset over the confrontation with Rita? she wondered. Maybe it was because she knew she hadn't tried to take Chad away from her. Not because she wasn't attracted to him, of course.

This morning when she'd awakened to his smile, she'd felt wonderful. It had taken her embarrassment to shake her from that enjoyment.

Now, of course, she remembered all the reasons to avoid Chad Randall. But she had enjoyed those few moments.

She unlocked and swung open the door, prepared to ignore Rita if she was still there.

She wasn't.

Chad was.

"What are you doing in here?" she demanded.

"I heard Rita berating you and thought I should rescue you." He grinned. "Want to reward me with a kiss?"

"No, I do not!" she protested, but she couldn't help smiling back. "But I do thank you. She seems to feel that I've stolen something from her. Namely, you."

"You couldn't steal what she didn't have. I've explained that to her."

Her gaze met his in surprise. "How did she take it?"

"Not well. She's downstairs right now demanding to be taken to the airport."

Megan's gaze turned to the window, noting that the storm hadn't let up. "I guess Jake's trying to explain to her why that's impossible."

"That would be my guess." Without any warning, he walked over and wrapped his arms around her. "Mmm, you smell good."

"Chad!" she exclaimed, taken by surprise. "What are you doing?"

"Giving you a morning hug. After sleeping together, I don't think that's too forward, do you?"

She pushed her way out of his embrace. "You're being ridiculous. We didn't sleep together."

"We most assuredly did. Unfortunately that's all we did...sleep." He followed her to the dresser where she was searching for socks.

"You shouldn't be in here," she told him, her fingers shaking as she finally pulled out a matching pair. He was unnerving her.

"What difference does it make? It's not like we're naked on the bed."

Megan frantically tried to dismiss the picture he'd drawn, but his fingers on her shoulders made it difficult. With her breathing becoming more and more shallow, she pulled away and sat down on the bed to pull on her socks.

Chad leaned against the dresser, his arms crossed over his broad chest, and watched her. "I've never thought putting on socks was sexy, but you've changed my mind, Meggie."

"Stop it!" She yanked on the second sock and stood. "I'm sure Red has breakfast ready. I don't want to keep him waiting."

"Where are your shoes?"

She looked around her, but concentration escaped her with Chad watching her every move. "I don't know!" she wailed.

He crossed to her side and hugged her again. "Shh, honey, don't get upset. You probably left them downstairs. Come on. We'll get them before we go to breakfast."

WITH HER SHOES RETRIEVED from the TV room and a big breakfast in her stomach, Megan felt much more in control of things an hour later. Even more so because Jake had given Chad a list of chores to be done.

When Chad was in the same room, she had difficulty concentrating. She hoped the storm ended soon. If not, she feared constant exposure to whatever chemistry occurred when she was with him would result in her doing something stupid. Like loving him.

"More coffee, Megan?" Red asked, interrupting her thoughts.

"Oh, yes, thanks, Red. But you didn't need to wait on me. I could've gotten it myself."

"Well, I thought I'd have a second cup with you."

Megan waited as Red joined her, wondering if he wanted to say something to her. However, he simply sipped his coffee, remaining silent.

"How much longer do you think the storm will last?" she finally asked.

"Reckon another day or two. You're not anxious to leave, are you?"

She smiled, hoping he wouldn't notice the tension she was feeling. "I've enjoyed my visit, but I have a job to do, you know."

"Are you one of these career ladies?" he asked, watching her intently, innocently repeating a question she'd been asked last night.

"I—I have to support myself, Red. And I like what I do."

He grunted in response and looked away. "Well, I wanted to tell you that havin' you here has made a real difference. We've been without any women for a long time. I kinda like a little feminine influence."

Neither of them had noticed Jake at the door. "Glad to hear you say that, Red. Megan will be back a lot to fix up the house. Her and Adele. And then there's the vet and her aunt. We're going to have women all over the place."

Megan looked at Jake, wondering if he knew that Chad had told them of his plan. She didn't think so. What would he think up next? Had his brothers figured out that he would come up with another scheme when this one didn't work?

"Red said he thought the storm would last another couple of days," she said, hoping Jake might have better news.

"If Red says so, then he's probably right. He's more accurate than the weatherman on television," Jake said as he poured himself a cup of coffee and settled down at the table.

"I'm going to sit down with Adele and put the final touches on our recommendation this morning," Megan told Jake. "Then, when the storm stops, you'll be able to ship us off at once."

"You make it sound like we're going to be glad to get rid of you," Jake drawled, smiling at her. "Red was right. We've enjoyed having some ladies around the place.''

Megan took a sip of coffee. Then she impulsively said, "Look, Jake, it's not going to work."

Both men stared at her, Red in puzzlement, but Jake's gaze grew hard.

"What are you talking about?"

"I know about your plan. I overheard Chad telling his brothers last night." As soon as she said the words, she wished she'd kept her thoughts to herself.

"Chad told them what?"

She finally lifted her gaze to his. "That you hired decorators because you hoped to—to matchmake."

"Damn his hide, that boy's got a big mouth."

"What's she talkin' about, Jake?" Red demanded. "You mean you're not gonna redo the kitchen?"

The sight of this wizened old cowboy worrying about his kitchen caused a bubble of laughter to escape. She was relieved when Jake's smile matched her own.

"Sure, we're going to redo the kitchen for you, Red. We're going to redo the whole blasted house, right, Megan?"

She nodded. "But we don't have to do the entire house, Jake. You could just choose part of our recommendations."

"Then what was she talkin' about it not workin'?" Red was persistent.

"Megan's talking about my plan to find wives for those three scalawags I call brothers." Jake smiled ruefully at her. "It was a kind of crazy plan, wasn't it?"

Megan shrugged her shoulders. "It might have worked, Jake," she said softly. "You were a little unlucky, that's all. You four Randall brothers are prime choice. The women in Denver would have a feeding frenzy if they knew about you."

"But not you?"

She ignored his question. "Pete's not ready to think about another woman. I think he's still hung up on Janie."

"You got that right," Red inserted.

"I've got two other brothers. Care to take either of them off my hands?"

With perfect timing, the back door opened and Chad and Pete rushed in.

Chapter Fourteen

"It's mighty cold out there." Pete shook off the snow and rubbed his hands together. "Got a spare cup of hot coffee, Red?"

"Sure do." The old man filled two more mugs.

"You've finished all the chores?" Jake asked his two brothers.

"Yeah." Chad took the seat beside Megan.

"How's Black Sugar?" she asked, breathing in the mixture of cold air and masculine scent that covered him.

"Looking good. He's not as wobbly this morning. B.J. was in the barn when I got there, checking him out." Chad smiled at his big brother. "I think Pete did a damn fine job of hiring a vet."

Jake grunted. "How's her family settling in? The boy and her aunt."

"She hasn't said," Chad replied, "but she told me yesterday that her husband was killed in a storm. Makes her boy nervous when she's out in bad weather."

In a casual move, he stretched his arm across the back of Megan's chair and drank his coffee with his left hand. Though she liked the warmth that surrounded her, she leaned forward, away from him, and sipped her coffee.

Jake frowned but said nothing.

"Aren't you going to offer us a snack?" Pete complained to Red, changing the subject. "I've been working hard. I need some sustenance."

"You've only been out there an hour or two, boy. What's wrong with you?" Red asked. But even with his question, he got up from the table.

"If you're going to serve cookies, I've got to leave," Megan said with a grin. She pushed her chair back, dislodging Chad's arm. "Any more of those cookies, and I won't be able to fit in my jeans."

"And that would be a real shame," Chad said softly, his grin cocky.

She glared at him before turning to Jake. "I'll go get together with Adele. We should be able to show you what we have in mind this afternoon."

"Great. I'll look forward to it," Jake assured her with a warm smile.

In fact, they were all smiling at her as she left the room, giving her a feeling of belonging. And one smile did more than that. It made her hot.

CHAD HAD RETURNED to the horse barn after a quiet lunch. Rita had decided to take all her meals in her room until it was possible to escape from the ranch.

Red agreed to her request because, as he put it, that was a lot less trouble than having that blasted woman in his kitchen.

Megan and Adele were meeting with Jake this afternoon to go over their proposal, so Chad knew he wouldn't see her. He might as well check on his horses.

He spent the afternoon puttering around the barn, cleaning the stalls, polishing tack...and thinking about Megan. The woman turned him on like no one else ever had. If she were leaving permanently when the snowstorm ended, he'd have to make a decision about his feelings, his desire, soon.

But she'd be back. He had time to work out the fascination he felt for her. Time to gain control of the need that was building in him. A need that scared him spitless.

Even during his early romantic escapades, he'd never felt so out of control, so needy. Yeah, he had time to step back and strengthen his resistance.

He was feeling pretty good about his decision until the barn door opened and a snow-covered Megan came in. He watched her from the shadows where he sat mending a bridle, his body tensing.

"Chad?" she called.

"Yeah. What are you doing out here?"

His voice gave away his position, and she walked toward him. "I wanted to see the babies again."

"Didn't anyone tell you you shouldn't come out in this storm without a good reason?"

"The storm isn't as bad now. It's still snowing, but the wind has died down." She tilted her head to one side, staring at him. "Are you in a bad mood?"

"Nope. How did the session with Jake go? You get the job?" He watched as she turned away from him, moving to the door of the nearest stall to pet the mare kept there.

"Yes. We're going to do the work in stages."

"So when will you be back?"

She looked over her shoulder at him. "I haven't left yet."

"I know. But you'll leave as soon as the storm's over, won't you?" Somehow, saying that fact aloud made his gut tighten.

"I suppose so."

"You like living in the city?"

Shrugging her shoulders, she murmured, "It's okay."

"Brett tried it. He couldn't stand it longer than a year."

"And you?"

"Only when I was in college."

"But according to Brett and Pete, you go to town a lot, at least on the weekends."

He smiled slightly. "A man gets tired of masculine company all the time."

"Ah."

"You seeing anyone?" Pete had already asked that question, but he wanted to hear her answer again.

She turned and wandered farther away from him to the next stall. "No."

"Why not?"

She shrugged her shoulders again.

"You're not being very talkative." He didn't think he'd ever complained about a woman not talking before. But he wanted to know everything about Megan.

Instead of answering him, she walked toward him. "What are you doing?"

"Mending a bridle."

"Oh. It's almost dinnertime."

"Yeah." More brilliant conversation. Finally he decided to stop avoiding the topic on his mind. "What are we going to do about this?"

"This what?"

"This feeling. I want you so bad that if you said the word, I'd strip you naked right here." A visible shiver ran over her, and he felt his body responding.

"I don't think that would be a good idea."

"Oh, it'd be a great idea. We might be a little late for dinner, but that's okay." His gaze roamed her body, even though more than half of it was covered by her coat.

"Stop it, Chad. I don't bed-hop."

"You said you weren't dating anyone!" he protested sharply.

"I'm not. But that doesn't mean I'm ready to jump in bed with you."

She wouldn't meet his gaze. "I'll wait," he finally said.

"For what?"

"Until you're ready. You'll be coming back real soon. I'll be here waiting."

"Why?"

He stared at her as if she'd lost her mind. "I just told you why. I want you. And I think you want me, too."

"I might not be back that often. You should find someone around here. There were some other women at that restaurant we visited."

He was irritated that she wouldn't admit she wanted him, that she kept shoving him toward other women. "Maybe you're right. Maybe I'll find a real woman, one who is willing to admit attraction when she feels it. One who doesn't hide behind her past."

"Look who's talking!" Her voice rose in irritation. "You and your brothers have let the past completely dominate your lives."

"Look, lady," he roared, "we were doing all right before you got here. We don't need you to point out our shortcomings."

"Well, the same is true for me," she yelled back, taking a step toward him. "I'm perfectly happy in Denver."

"And I'm perfectly happy right here. Without you!" he lied as he cast aside the bridle and stood. Then he grabbed her shoulders and pulled her against him, his mouth covering hers before she could protest.

Her lips were warm and pliant, molding to his, opening to his urging. Chad felt the pressure build in his body as they came together. She'd unbuttoned her coat earlier, and his hands slid around her inside it, pressing her closer. Her arms encircled his neck, her fingers weaving through his hair.

He felt as if he were going to explode. Never had he gotten so hot so fast. His hands slid beneath her sweater, stroking her satiny skin, loving the feel of it beneath his fingers. Breaking the kiss to gasp for breath, he muttered her name several times, drinking in her beautiful face. But he couldn't last long without her kisses.

Megan was drowning in sensations. Everywhere he touched her, she felt on fire. His kisses seemed as necessary to her existence as air and water, and she pressed closer, enjoying feeling buried in his strength. But she wanted more.

She wanted to be one with Chad. The attraction she'd felt the first time he touched her had grown, expanded at a rapid rate. When she'd awakened in his arms this morning, she felt as if she'd come home. As if she finally belonged. As if she'd be there forever.

Desire racked her body, causing her to tremble against his hardness. He pushed up her sweater as his hands sought her breasts, cupping, stroking them. She pressed closer, only wanting more of his touch.

He whispered her name as he lifted her against him to caress her breasts. Even as she clung to him, she wanted the same privilege, to touch his skin. When he lowered her to a pile of hay and began undressing her, she unbuttoned his shirt and slid her fingers over his hard chest, loving the feel of him.

Chad's mouth returned to hers, as a parched man to the well. Any conscious thought went spinning away. All she could do was cling, stroke, consume and be consumed in return. She became lost in a world filled with Chad.

He undid her jeans and slid them down, along with her panties. As impatient as he, she assisted him in unbuttoning his jeans, too. The power and strength of him only made her long for him even more.

When he pulled away from her, the loss was almost more than she could bear. "Chad?"

"Just a minute, Meggie," he whispered, his breathing rapid. When she realized he was preparing to protect her, removing a condom from his jeans, not stop loving her, she lay back and waited. Without his touch, sanity began to return. What was she doing? She couldn't— Before she could complete that thought, Chad's lips were covering hers again and taking her to incredible heights of pleasure.

When he entered her, neither could wait for completion. Mindlessly they each urged the other to that unique journey of two souls.

When their rasping breaths had softened to normal breathing again, Megan delighted in Chad's heavy warmth and a sense of peace that filled her. Had she found her home? Had Chad been as devastated by their lovemaking as she? She longed to ask him what the past few moments had meant to him, but she was afraid. Though she called herself a coward, she remained silent.

"Sorry, Megan. I didn't intend for that to happen."

Chad's rough whisper cut her to the quick. He was apologizing for their lovemaking.

He stood and pulled up his jeans, refastening them as he turned his back to her. Feeling like some discarded souvenir, she, too, stood, dressing as she did so.

"Me, neither." What else could she say? Afraid she'd burst into tears any moment, she grabbed her coat, shrugging into it as she moved and ran from the barn, ignoring Chad's call.

CHAD DIDN'T RETURN to the house right away. He needed time to compose himself . . . and to decide what he should do.

After promising himself he'd take time to get his needs under control, he'd blown it. He'd wanted Megan so bad, he'd made love to her on the hard floor, pleasuring himself without any thought of her.

Not that she hadn't wanted it as bad as him. He was sure of that. But he'd wanted their first time together to be special. Instead, he'd taken her on a haystack with her clothes half-on.

The tension that had sizzled between them since the day she arrived had short-circuited his system today. He only hoped she would let him show her how generous a lover he could be. Especially since even the thought of loving Megan again made him hard.

Finally he made his way to the house, wondering if Megan would make an appearance at dinner. Wondering if she'd talk to him. Wondering if he'd ever kiss her again.

Dear God, he hoped so.

His first question was answered at once.

Everyone was gathered around the table, staring at him as he entered. His gaze flew straight to Megan, and she turned a bright red. And looked more desirable than ever.

"We was beginning to worry about you," Red said. "Come on, boy, you're holding up dinner."

Chad washed at the sink and took his seat beside Adele, his gaze remaining on Megan.

"Everything okay in the horse barn?" Jake asked after saying the blessing.

"Uh, yeah," Chad muttered, distracted by the bowl of mashed potatoes Adele was passing him. "Sorry. I didn't realize it was so late."

"How's the storm looking?" Pete asked.

Chad stared at him blankly. The storm? The storm he remembered had taken place between him and Megan. And right now it felt just as cold. "I—I think it's letting up."

"Then if we get out early in the morning with the snowplow, ladies, you might be able to catch an afternoon flight to Denver," Jake said. "After dinner we'll check the forecasts and call for reservations."

Chad wanted to protest. But he couldn't figure out a good reason. He stared at Megan, but she concentrated on her food. He noticed, however, that she only picked at it, shifting it around the plate instead of eating.

"You off your feed?" Red asked, and Chad looked up, expecting him to be speaking to Megan. Instead, he was staring at Chad.

"Who, me? No! No, I was just thinking." He took a big bite of steak and chewed determinedly, his gaze drawn back to Megan.

"I checked with the men in the bunkhouse, and they'll be out at first light to see to the herds. Chad, you and Brett had better go out with them. Pete and I will clear things out here and get the ladies to the airport." Jake never looked up as he ordered their day.

"No!" Chad protested without thinking. When everyone at the table stared at him, he added, "I can handle the snowplow better than Pete. It broke down the last time he used it. Remember, Pete?" He stared desperately at his brother, hoping he'd understand.

"Oh, yeah, right," Pete said after meeting Chad's gaze. "You'd better do the snowplowing. I'll go chase cows." There was a thud from under the table as Pete turned to Jake. "That's okay with you, Jake, isn't it?"

Chad didn't know if Pete had kicked Jake or not, but he breathed a sigh of relief when his oldest brother looked at him and agreed. "Good idea. We wouldn't want the snowplow to break down tomorrow."

Brett stared at all of them, a puzzled look on his face. "I don't remember the plow breaking down."

"Doesn't matter," Chad hurriedly assured him, avoiding Megan's eyes now, in case she caught on to his scheme.

He didn't understand how he could be so vulnerable to this woman. He hadn't known her that long, but every moment around her was precious. He'd figured once they'd made love, his hunger for her would ease. But he'd been wrong. He wanted her more than ever.

He cleared his throat. "Well, I hate to sound like a certain blonde, but what are we going to do this evening?"

Adele expressed enthusiasm, commenting on how much she'd enjoyed forty-two that first night, which seemed like weeks ago to Chad. He looked at Megan again. "Megan? Will you be my partner?"

She kept her gaze on her plate. "Thank you anyway, but I believe I'd better go pack. And I have a few more additions to the plans we've made. Red, I like your idea about making a mud room."

"Yesiree, that mud room will keep my kitchen a lot cleaner."

Adele was more interested in the forty-two game. "Jake, will you and Pete make up the foursome? I'd really love to play."

"Of course. We'll be glad to join you and Chad."

Chad wanted to groan in his misery. Now he was trapped in a game of forty-two that would go on all night while Megan escaped. Maybe he'd be able to persuade Brett to take his place. But he couldn't ask until they were away from the table.

After that, conversation languished. And Chad thought everyone and everything moved in slow motion, while his heart raced at double speed. He felt he somehow had to talk with Megan tonight, to find out how she felt about what had happened.

When she excused herself from the table, he willed her to meet his gaze, to give him some encouragement. Instead, she left the room without even telling him good-night.

"You do something to Megan to upset her?" Jake asked as soon as the door closed behind her.

Chad looked up to find Jake staring at him. And shook his head no. It wasn't exactly a lie. She hadn't been upset until after they'd made love.

"Okay, then," Jake said, standing. "Let's go play some forty-two."

Chad had no choice but to join the game. But he was going to talk to Megan tonight. She wasn't getting away until they settled what had happened between them.

Chapter Fifteen

It took Megan all of fifteen minutes to pack.

What was she going to do the rest of the evening?

She paced the floor, trying not to think about what had happened in the barn. Trying not to remember Chad's touch. The man was all wrong for her. There was no future in their passion.

But there was a lot of heat.

"Stop it, Megan!" she ordered herself. Woman could not live by sex alone, she paraphrased. And Chad had made it clear he had no interest in a permanent relationship.

And she didn't, either, she hurriedly reminded herself. She'd watched her mother ride a roller coaster of heartbreak and passion. Even worse, she'd been an innocent passenger on the ride. She wouldn't do the same thing to a child of her own because Chad made her want him.

Already, after sleeping with him once, she knew it wouldn't be enough. She couldn't keep any distance, any perspective, if she was around him. She would lose all control—as she had in the barn.

And that frightened her most of all. Loss of control made a person vulnerable to another's whims.

She opened the door and cautiously peered into the hallway. Maybe she could find something to read without going into the living room, where Chad was playing. She'd go crazy if she couldn't keep her mind off him.

Walking softly, she headed for the kitchen, but found it empty. As she came back into the hallway, she heard the television. Easing open the door to the room, she saw Brett all alone watching the big screen.

"Brett, would you mind some company?" she asked.

"Of course not," he replied, smiling over his shoulder. "That is, unless you want me to change the channel. This is one of my favorite shows," he explained, gesturing to the sitcom.

"No, I like this program, too." She settled down on the sofa beside him and tried to lose herself in the story.

She was only partly successful. The banter between the couple on-screen, flirting madly with each other, made her think of Chad. The kiss they shared stirred her passions and made her shift uncomfortably on the sofa.

"Need more room?" Brett asked without looking at her.

"No, I'm fine." She willed herself not to move.

When the program ended, Brett offered her a choice of a romance or a detective show. She chose the detective program. She'd rather see someone get shot than kissed tonight. It would be less bothersome.

Halfway through the hour-long show, Brett suggested they have a snack. Though she wasn't hungry, Megan accompanied him to the kitchen. She wasn't willing to remain alone outside her bedroom this evening. Chad might find her.

Just as they were ready to return to the TV room with their leftover apple pie and coffee, the door swung open and Chad stared at them.

"What are you doing here?" he demanded.

Megan tried to ignore him, but when she walked past him, he grabbed her arm. "I thought you had to pack."

"I did. Excuse me."

But he wouldn't let her escape that easily. "Come play forty-two."

"No, thank you. Please turn loose of my arm."

He didn't move, staring at her.

"Come on, Chad, let the lady go. Our show is starting again," Brett complained.

"You're watching television?"

"Yes, we are." Megan yanked her arm free and hurried out the door, afraid he'd follow. If he did, she'd be relegated to her lonely room again.

"What's going on between you and Chad?" Brett asked once they were seated again.

She almost choked on her bite of pie. "What do you mean?"

"Come on, Megan. Anyone can see you react to each other. Kind of like two hot wires touching. Sparks fly. You interested in him?"

"Do you remember our discussion last night? Neither of us is interested in anything permanent. And I don't do one-nighters," she said crisply, her gaze determinedly fixed on the television, hoping he couldn't tell she just had.

"Chad's a good guy," Brett explained, "but he took Jake's divorce about as hard as Jake. We all love Jake, but I think Chad almost idolizes him."

Megan looked at the handsome man beside her. "Just because Jake's marriage failed doesn't mean yours or your brothers' would fail. Not that I'm interested in—in anything like that. But if Jake tried romance again, he might find things changed."

Brett laughed. "You may be right. But if there's one thing we can all count on, it's Jake not trying marriage again. He's a hardheaded cuss."

"I think it runs in the family," she said dryly, and turned back to the television. Watching someone else suffer was easier than continuing their discussion.

CHAD MENTALLY KICKED himself over and over again. Megan was sitting in the room across the hall with Brett, and he was trapped at the game table. How could he have been such an idiot?

"Chad, you just trumped your partner's trick," Jake reprimanded mildly.

"Oh, sorry, Pete." He was grateful when Pete sent him a sympathetic look.

"No problem. These sharks were gonna take us anyway," he said, gesturing to Jake and Adele.

"We're just having a good run of luck," Adele said.

Which was more than he was doing, Chad decided. He was determined to talk to Megan tonight, *had* to talk to her tonight—though his body wanted to do a lot more than talk.

Just thinking about what he'd like to do with Megan caused a reaction. He hunched over the table, hoping no one would notice, and tried to concentrate on the dominoes.

Good manners insisted, as well as Jake's stern eye, that Chad remain at the table until their guest had her fill of the game. He played quickly, preferring speed to skill, hoping the number of games racked up by Jake and Adele would satisfy her.

Around ten o'clock, he heard voices in the hallway and realized Brett and Megan were going upstairs. He lost all concentration at the thought.

"Your play, Chad," Jake ordered.

"Uh, what was led?"

"Fives," Pete answered with a grin. As if he'd read Chad's mind, he added, "Threes are trumps."

"I think that might be considered table talk, boys," Jake muttered, glaring at Chad.

He kept his gaze on his dominoes, trying to think about the game instead of a certain young woman going to her bedroom, taking off her clothes, brushing her hair—

"Chad!" Jake barked. "Pay attention."

He'd misplayed again. With a sigh, he offered his apologies for his boneheaded play.

As they finished the hand, Adele pushed back from the table. "It's late. I know you three worked a lot harder than I did today, so why don't we turn in?"

Chad could've hugged her. "I am a little tired," he muttered, smiling his gratitude at Adele. "I'll put things away," he added. He'd have to wait until everyone was settled down for the night before he could go to Megan's door.

And hope she didn't yell for him to go away.

"Want any help?" Pete asked as Jake and Adele left the room.

"Nope, but thanks for putting up with me tonight."

Pete grinned. "You tolerated my bad moods the past couple of weeks, didn't you?"

"But you're feeling better. You haven't been so down since the ladies arrived," Chad declared. He wanted Pete to recover from his heartbreak. Chad needed to believe recovery was possible. For him, too.

"Yeah, sure."

"Unless Janie walked in the door?" Chad prodded ruefully, having heard the doubt in Pete's voice.

"That's not going to happen, so we don't have to worry about it. Good night, little brother."

Pete really had it bad. Sighing, Chad admitted he might be in as much trouble as his brother. That was a frightening thought.

He cleaned up and ran upstairs for a quick shower. In clean jeans and a flannel shirt that he left untucked, he opened the bathroom door and listened intently.

When he heard nothing, he tiptoed out into the hallway, pulling his door to behind him. He felt like a teenager, trying to sneak in past his curfew. Reaching Megan's door undetected, he rapped softly.

No response.

Could she be asleep already? It'd only been half an hour since he'd heard her come upstairs. Time enough for someone to fall asleep, unless she had something on her mind.

Like that encounter in the barn.

He rapped again. She couldn't be asleep yet. When he heard the slightest sound of movement beyond the door, he leaned against the doorjamb in relief.

"Who's there?" she called softly.

"Chad. We need to talk."

"No. We'll talk in the morning."

"Megan, there won't be time. Let me in."

"No," she whispered back.

But he wasn't accepting that answer. Without warning, he turned the doorknob, hoping she hadn't locked her door. It silently swung open, and he slipped into the room.

"Chad!" she protested in a hoarse whisper, moving rapidly away from the door. "You can't come in here. What if someone hears you?"

"They won't. Everyone's gone to bed." He moved toward her, but she continued to back away until she was pressed against the wall by the window.

He halted suddenly, remembering their discussion in B.J.'s house that first day. Instead, he just repeated his entreaty. "Meggie, we need to talk."

"About what?"

"How about the fact that you drive me crazy? I played forty-two like the village idiot tonight. Jake was ready to slug me."

She looked away. "I don't think I can be blamed for your poor play."

"Probably not. But my body reacts to yours like steel to a magnet. I can't resist the pull." He stepped closer again. "Just like now. I want to touch you so badly my body aches from holding back."

"We—we can't touch. It would be a disaster. We both know we have a problem. You'd better go to your room before we lose control." Her hands were clasped tightly in front of her, as if she didn't trust them.

"I think it may be too late. I'm afraid I'll start drooling if I don't get to kiss you soon," he said with a grin, trying a little humor to lighten the mood.

"Ugh. Very unattractive," she agreed, smiling in return.

"I can't think of anything that would make you unattractive, Meggie. Don't you see? We need to explore what's going on here. Neither of us could stop this afternoon. Whatever it is, it's pretty strong."

"You apologized."

Chad frowned, trying to figure out what her statement meant. "Yeah?"

"If you regretted it this afternoon, what makes you think now would be any better?

With a lopsided grin, he confessed, "Honey, I didn't apologize because it wasn't good. If it got any better, I'd die." Her cheeks flamed, and he wanted to pull her into his arms. "I apologized because I wanted it to be right for you."

She licked her lips, and Chad thought he was going to fall to his knees. "Don't do that."

"What?" she asked, startled.

He leaned forward and lightly touched his tongue to her bottom lip. Her hands came up to frame his face, but her fingers were shaking against his skin.

"Meggie, I can't stand this torment any longer. We want each other. We're both adults," he breathed, his mouth only inches from hers.

Suddenly Megan capitulated, closing the distance between them, her mouth taking his, her arms pulling him closer.

Not that Chad resisted. Once she'd shown her willingness, he devoured her with his lips, his arms, his entire body. Unlike this afternoon in the barn, when she'd been covered with a lot of clothes, tonight she was dressed in the same thigh-length silky robe and nightgown she'd been wearing the morning he'd brought her breakfast.

With eager hands, he slipped the robe from her shoulders while his mouth continued to caress hers. Their breaths mingled, and he could scarcely contain his desire to make love to her again.

"Meggie," he whispered, burying his face in her neck, his lips touching her skin. "I want to eat you alive."

Her fingers began working the buttons on his shirt, and soon her hot hands were stroking his chest, her fingers burrowing through the hair on his chest, rubbing his nipples with lightning touches.

His fingers slid to the hem of her gown, and he slipped it over her head. "It's only fair play," he assured her teasingly, his hands imitating hers.

Her breathing quickened, and his mouth covered hers again, as if to help her breathe. Their tongues parried and thrust while his hands wandered over her enticing figure. Chill bumps on her back gave him an excuse to move them to the bed.

"You need to be under the covers, sweetheart," he managed to say, his chest heaving as he yanked back the bedspread and eased her down on the mattress. He was reassured when her arms reached up to him, urging him to join her. Before he did so, he removed his jeans and briefs, then reached for her panties.

One part of him wanted to stand and admire her beauty. The other urged him closer. He slipped into bed beside her, loving the warmth she exuded against the entire length of his body.

He needed no encouragement to be ready to make her his. All it took was being within a mile of her and he was ready. As she whispered, "Please, oh please, Chad," in his ear, he moved over her, eager to please her.

Only then did he remember the condom he'd put in his jeans. Premeditation, he knew, but Jake had drummed responsibility into all their heads. "Wait, Meggie. I need protection."

She said nothing as he prepared himself, but there was no waning of desire when he returned to her side. Her mouth joined his again, and her body welcomed his touch.

When he entered her, her warmth closing around him, there was a second's peace, a momentary exaltation that filled him with greater happiness than he'd ever known. Then an urgency drove him, and he and Megan joined together in soul-shattering satisfaction.

When his heart slowed to a steady thud, he eased himself to the mattress beside her, then wrapped his arms around her to pull her close. "Are you all right, Meggie?" he whispered.

"Yes. Yes, I—I'm fine. You?"

He pressed her even closer to him. "I'm better than I've ever been in my life." The words he'd never said to a woman hovered in his mind, and he resisted the inexplicable urge to whisper those fatal words, *I love you.*

He was moved by the moment, he reasoned. If he said something like that now, she wouldn't believe him anyway. Hell, he didn't believe himself, he thought staunchly even as he held her against him.

One of her hands stole to his chest, her fingers playing against his skin.

"Didn't get enough before?" he whispered, his lips punctuating his question with kisses on her neck.

"I like to touch you," she whispered in return.

He pulled back to study her face, but she buried it in his chest, apparently unwilling to look at him.

"Meggie? Are you all right?"

"You already asked me that. I'm fine." Her hand trailed down his chest, heading in a dangerous direction.

Already his body was gearing up for a repeat performance, which pleased and startled him, but also brought problems. He'd only brought one condom with him.

Her lips were nibbling at his neck, sending shivers all over his body, and his hands cupped her hips, pulling her against him.

"Meggie," he whispered, desperately trying to control his response to her. "You'd better get to sleep. Tomorrow's going to be a long day."

There was a sudden stillness after he spoke. Then her hand withdrew from his body, and she turned her face away from his. "Yes, I am tired."

"Meggie," he pleaded without being sure what he was pleading for, "I don't want you to be embarrassed if someone sees me leaving your room. Jake gets up early."

"That's very thoughtful of you."

The words were fine. Her tone of voice wasn't.

He pulled her head back toward him and kissed her again, but her lips were cold, and her heart wasn't in the caress. He didn't know what to do. His first instinct was to make fierce love to her, convincing her he wanted her. But to do so unprotected would be wrong.

He had to leave. Even thinking about making love to her again had him pulsing with desire. "I'll see you in the morning."

He forced himself to slide from the covers and pick up his clothing. He slipped on the jeans but didn't bother with the shirt. Then he bent to kiss her one more time. She turned her head away just as his lips reached her face, and he touched her cheek.

"Good night," she murmured, her eyes closed.

"Good night," he returned, but he stared at her, frowning, rather than leaving at once. She never moved. He crossed to the door, looking at her once more.

An unsatisfying ending to a very satisfying night.

MEGAN DIDN'T OPEN her eyes until she heard the door close. When she did look, she was glad to discover the room empty, because the tears that had gathered behind her eyelids now ran down her face.

So, a good time was had by all.

And that was that.

Chad had more mundane thoughts than the paradise he'd just shared with her. There was potential embarrassment and the need for sleep. Maybe the problem was their lovemaking hadn't meant to him what it had to her. She'd known it would be a mistake to get so close to Chad. And she was right.

After all her warnings to herself, she'd laid her heart on the line one more time. And again it was trampled. There was no protection left to her. She couldn't pretend he didn't matter to her.

She loved him. Totally. Completely. With all her heart. And he was concerned about embarrassment.

He wanted to hide what had happened from everyone. She wanted to shout it from the rooftop. What had happened between them had been the most glorious event in her life—and would lead to the most incredible heartache.

And perhaps even cost her her job.

She couldn't come back to the Randall ranch now. The decorating would have to be done by someone else in her firm. Or maybe Adele by herself. Megan just knew she couldn't return to Chad's home. She would come as a beggar, pleading for his love, his touch, even a smile.

What they had, what they'd shared tonight, would turn into a sleazy affair, with Chad eventually returning to his other women. Wherever he found them.

Better to cut off her association with the Randalls now and do what she could to protect her poor over-worked heart. She couldn't avoid the pain, but maybe she could shorten it.

Too bad her decision only brought more tears.

Chapter Sixteen

Chad was in the kitchen at first light. "No time for breakfast, Red. I'll grab a cup of coffee and be on my way."

"What's the hurry, boy?"

"I want to be back and have breakfast with Meg— the ladies. I figure I can put in a couple of hours' work before then."

Red gave him a knowing grin. "I see."

He was on his way out of the house as Jake entered the kitchen.

"Chad wants to get a head start," Red said behind him.

Chad grinned. That would make Jake suspicious, for sure. Chad wasn't at his best in the mornings, though he could think of circumstances where waking up would be a pleasure.

For example, if he were in bed with Megan.

He regretted leaving her last night. Her response hadn't been reassuring. Had she been offended that he'd left? He didn't think she'd want everyone to know what had happened last night. For himself, he was ready to tell the world that Megan Chase was his woman.

The world. Denver. She was returning to Denver without him. No one in Denver would know she was his. Maybe he'd need to make a trip to Denver real soon. Yeah, that's what he'd do. She'd probably be back here in a month. So if he visited Denver in a couple of weeks, the wait wouldn't be so long.

Though his plans pleased him, he noticed they didn't satisfy the uneasiness he was feeling. He wasn't sure of the source of that uneasiness, but he thought it had something to do with the way he'd left Megan last night.

Driving the snowplow at a speed Jake wouldn't approve of, Chad turned back to the house after an hour and a half, with one lane clear to the road. He was anxious to see Megan.

When he burst into the kitchen, the table was full, Jake, Red, Adele and even Rita around the table. But no Megan.

"Hi, guess I'm in time. Where's Megan?"

"I knocked on her door," Adele assured him. "She said she'd be right down."

Chad gave her a smile and headed for the stairway. Bounding up the stairs two at a time, he rounded the corner to Megan's room just as the door opened.

"I thought maybe you'd overslept," Chad teased with a grin. She had a surprised look on her face, her full lips parted, her eyes rounded.

He didn't hesitate. The need to taste her again, to feel her against him, was so overwhelming he swept her into his arms. To his relief, she responded at once, her mouth opening to his, her arms around his neck.

"Wanna skip breakfast?" he whispered, his lips trailing down her neck. He noticed she wasn't wearing his favorite, jeans. Today she was the professional decorator again, clad in a suit and heels.

"I—I'm hungry. And we have to leave soon, don't we?" she asked breathlessly.

"Yeah," he reluctantly agreed, allowing her to take a step back. "You okay this morning?" She didn't meet his gaze as she straightened her suit jacket.

"I'm fine. We'd better go down. I'm late already." She started around him, but he caught her hand.

"There's not that big a rush," he assured her, and brought her hand to his lips. He frowned as she turned away from him and pulled him toward the stairs.

As quickly as she moved, he had to hurry to keep up. "Megan?" he questioned, but she never stopped.

As they reached the kitchen door, she pulled her hand from him and entered in front of him. Once they were at the table, he had no chance to talk to her, of course.

"Your travel agent called before any of you were up," Jake announced as they took their places. "She asked me to tell you she got you seats on the eleven-o'clock flight. We'll need to leave for the airport as soon as you finish breakfast."

"Wasn't there anything later?" Chad asked.

"Why would we want to hang around here?" Rita asked with bitterness in her voice.

Chad shrugged, but his gaze was on Megan. She concentrated on her breakfast.

Something was wrong. It didn't take a rocket scientist to figure that one out, Chad concluded. And whatever it was had gone wrong last night, when he'd left her bed.

He hoped Megan would return to her bedroom one last time and he could catch her there alone. Instead, Jake sent him and Red up for the luggage. When he came down, Megan was speaking to Jake alone.

Okay, so he'd sit beside her in the Suburban. They could whisper without anyone overhearing them. He stored the luggage and turned to offer a hand to each of the ladies as they entered the vehicle.

"Why don't you ride out and see how the others are doing? They might need a little help," Jake said, coming to a stop beside him.

"I thought I was going with you," Chad said, surprised.

Jake looked at him, a sympathetic stare that confused Chad. Then his brother began pulling on gloves, staring at his hands. "Megan asked that you not go," he said quietly.

Chad looked at his brother, then Megan. She'd been watching him, but as soon as he looked her way, she leaned forward to say something to Adele.

"She what?"

"Megan asked that you not come with us. She said she would be uncomfortable." Jake put a hand on his shoulder. "Maybe you can straighten things out the next time she comes."

Then he got behind the wheel, waved a hand at Chad and Red and pulled away.

Chad stood, as frozen as the ground under his feet, too shocked to even think.

"You want some more coffee before you ride out?" Red asked. When he didn't respond, the old man nudged him. "You want more coffee?"

"Yeah." Chad finally turned and walked into the kitchen. With every step he took, he had a growing certainty he'd just made a huge mistake.

MEGAN WORKED VERY HARD at keeping her composure all the way into Casper. It helped that she didn't need to make conversation.

When it came time to tell Jake goodbye, she thought she was going to be professional about it. Then he hugged her.

"We'll be looking forward to your return," he said softly as his big arms enfolded her. "You feel like part of the family."

"Oh, Jake," she said, half sigh, half cry, and one tear escaped to trail down her face.

"You call us if you need help, Megan, okay?"

She nodded and ran for the airplane gate. Call the Randalls? Not likely, though she knew she'd want to. But they were the problem, not the solution.

Adele took the seat next to her. "We just made it. The plane leaves in ten minutes."

She looked out the window, saying nothing. She was still too on edge to speak.

"Are you okay?"

Nodding, she gave a brief glance Adele's way and then turned back to the window. *Please take off. Please take off.* She repeated those words in her head over and over again, like a mantra that would save her.

The plane engines revved up, and she closed her eyes in thanks. Her ordeal was almost over. She would leave Wyoming and never return.

A commotion at the front of the plane caused her to open her eyes. She was suddenly consumed by fear that one of the Randalls would walk down the aisle. Instead, it was an elderly lady followed by an impatient attendant. Megan breathed a sigh of relief. She was being silly. She and the Randalls—*all* the Randalls— had parted company. This interlude in her life was over.

Completely over.

She tried not to cry again.

CHAD RAN THROUGH the airport. After having purchased his ticket, with the warning that the plane was ready to take off, he knew he had no time to spare.

Unfortunately a young mother with two small toddlers didn't know that. She'd allowed the smallest to wander right into Chad's path while she tended to the temper tantrum the older one was giving.

Chad's choice was to run over the child or come to a screeching halt and hope he wouldn't wipe out. He did his best to stop, but he scooped the child into his arms to protect him as he did so and set off a commotion as the mother assumed he was trying to kidnap her baby.

With the woman screaming so loudly that security guards came from all directions and the older child continuing his temper tantrum, Chad had no hope of catching his plane. In fact, he was going to be lucky if he didn't spend the night in jail.

After a long and tortuous explanation, and several phone calls, he was released.

With a determination that had only grown stronger with each moment since Megan's departure, he returned to the ticket counter. Too bad he hadn't come to his senses before she'd left.

By the time he had reached the kitchen for that cup of coffee Red had offered, Chad had known, with a surety that scared him, that if he didn't go after Megan then, right that minute, he might never see her again.

He couldn't let that happen.

With blinding quickness, he had also realized that if he didn't claim Megan Chase as his in every sense of the word, his life would be useless.

He thought back to his talk with Pete. He didn't want to make the mistakes Pete had made. Pete had lost the woman he loved.

Chad wasn't going to do the same thing.

When he landed in Denver, Chad, with no luggage, made a quick exit from the airport. He hailed a cab before he remembered he didn't have Megan's address. "Take me to the nearest phone booth with a directory," he ordered.

The driver frowned, but at least he didn't order Chad out of his taxi. "What you lookin' for?"

"A woman."

"No need for a phone directory. I can take you to the right place," the cabbie assured him with a wink, and swung his taxi into the traffic.

Chad shook his head. "No, not that kind of woman. I mean, a specific woman. I just need to look up her address. Then you can take me there."

The driver shrugged his shoulders. As soon as the taxi exited the airport, he pulled into a drive-in grocery and motioned to the phone booth next to it. "There you go. But you gotta pay me something afore you get out."

Chad whipped out his billfold and removed a twenty-dollar bill. "Here, this will be my deposit." He almost left the taxi before the cabbie's happy smile reminded him. "But you'd better not drive off without me, 'cause I'll report you if you do."

"Hey, man, I wouldn't do that," the driver protested, holding up his hands in innocence.

With that, Chad rushed to the phone book hanging by a chain. M. C. Chase, M. L. Chase and Marvin Chase were three possibilities. With a silent apology to all future seekers, he ripped the page out of the directory and returned to the cab.

He selected the first Chase—M.C.—as the most likely.

The taxi stopped in front of some expensive condos. "You want me to wait?" the driver asked hopefully.

Chad considered the question and then refused. Somehow he felt sure he'd found Megan's address. He paid the driver.

After checking the mailboxes, Chad raced up the stairs to the last apartment on the second floor. He rapped on the door and was relieved when Megan opened it and looked out at him through the small opening afforded by the chain.

"Megan, I need to talk to you," he said, but she stared at him in astonishment. When she didn't move, he said, "Megan, let me in."

"No!" she gasped, and slammed the door in his face.

He knocked again.

"You're not coming in, Chad," she shouted through the door.

"I just want to talk, Meggie. What's wrong with that?"

"I believe that's what you said last night before you came into my bedroom," she reminded him coldly.

Guilt filled him. She was right. That was exactly what he'd said.

He leaned against the door. "Megan, please."

"No!"

"Why? Why are you mad at me?" He felt ridiculous having a conversation with a closed door, but his choices were limited.

"I'm not mad. I—I don't want to see you anymore."

"Until you come back to the ranch?"

Silence. Panic gripped him.

"You're not planning to come back, are you?"

"Go away, Chad!"

"No, I won't." He wasn't sure exactly what to do. He only knew Megan was the most important person in the world to him.

He decided to wait.

WHAT WAS WRONG with the man?

Megan peeked out the front window for the tenth time, only to discover Chad still leaning against the wall, his arms crossed over his chest.

He must be freezing.

Finally she grabbed her coat and purse. She had to buy groceries. There was nothing in the house to eat. When she opened the door, he eagerly turned to face her.

"Go away!"

"No."

"I'm leaving."

"Where are you going?"

"To the grocery store."

"Mind if I come along? I'm kind of hungry."

She didn't say anything, but he must've taken her silence as a yes since he followed her down the stairs.

When she unlocked her car, he slid into the passenger seat and clipped his seat belt in place. The only sign that he'd been standing in subfreezing temperatures for half an hour was his appreciation of the heater.

"I'll run you back to the airport if you're ready," she said softly as he warmed his hands.

He looked at her sharply. "I'm not going anywhere."

"Chad, this is pointless."

"Is it?"

She turned in at the grocery store, not answering
him.

Pushing a cart, she hurried up and down the aisles,
not watching Chad. She didn't have to—as if by ra-
dar, she knew exactly where he was most of the time.
He picked up a few items in one of the small carryalls
and checked out before she reached the cash register.

He was waiting to carry her two bags when she was
finished.

They didn't speak all the way back to her apartment. At her door, he handed her the two bags without saying a word, taking up his sentinel position
against the wall.

"Chad, it gets almost as cold here as it does in
Wyoming. You're going to freeze."

"I'll manage. I'm not going anywhere until we talk,
Meggie. This is important."

"I don't want to talk," she insisted, trying to make
her voice sound firm. But she was afraid he'd heard it
waver. She slammed the door extrahard to convince
him.

After pacing her apartment for another twenty minutes, she opened the door again. "You can come in and
sleep on the couch. But I don't want to talk."

His nose was red, his hands were tucked under his
arms and the collar on his jacket was turned up around
his ears. But he shook his head no. "I'm not coming in

to sleep on the couch. I'm coming in to talk...and then to sleep in your bed. It's all or nothing, Megan. That's the way it has to be."

"Why, you—you conceited, arrogant, stubborn cowboy! Fine! Freeze to death! See if I care!" She slammed the door again. And slumped against it.

How long could she keep this up? She was fighting Chad...and she was fighting herself. What if she let him in? She *wanted* to love him again, to have him love her until the rest of the world disappeared, leaving only the two of them.

It was the heartache afterward that she couldn't face.

Just one more time, an insidious voice inside her whispered. *What can one more time hurt?*

Again she paced the living room, arguing with herself, sending angry looks at the door, as if Chad could sense her mood through the wood.

Finally, with the argument that she couldn't have his death on her hands, she swung the door open again. Prepared to let him in, to accept another night in his arms, to have the right to touch him, if only for twenty-four hours, she was shocked to find he'd gone.

CHAD WAITED with impatience for the phone to be answered. When his brother's voice finally spoke, he hurriedly said, "Jake, it's Chad. I guess Red told you I'm in Denver. I'm not sure when I'll be back."

"You okay?"

"Yeah. I have to get things straightened out with Megan."

"Call if you need us, little brother."

"I will. Thanks, Jake."

He hung up and hurried up the stairs to Megan's apartment, thinking as he walked how fortunate he was to have his family. He was almost to the apartment door when he realized Megan had come outside and now was disappearing again.

"Megan!" he called, and she hesitated. "I went to call Jake, to let him know where I was."

"I thought you'd gone," she said, her gaze meeting his for one unsettling look before she turned away.

"I told you I'm not going anywhere. Have you decided to talk to me?"

"I—I don't want you to freeze to death."

"I'll be okay."

"You can come in." Then, without looking at him, she nodded and went inside.

Chad picked up the sack full of his purchases from the store and followed her in.

Megan took his jacket from him. "You're freezing," she said. "Would you like something hot to drink?"

"No, that's not what I need to warm me up." He stood still, waiting for her to give him permission to touch her.

She swallowed, licked her lips and took a small step toward him. "Are you sure that's what you want?"

"With all my heart."

She melted into his arms, heat meeting ice, and Chad warmed up right away. Her kisses drove him wild in nothing flat. "Where's the bedroom, Meggie?"

All thought of talk went out of his mind, and evidently hers, too, since she showed him the way. He swept her up in his arms and hurried through the door she pointed out.

He almost didn't remember the bag in his hand. But as he laid her down on the bed, Jake's warnings reminded him. He removed the condoms he'd bought at the grocery store.

Shoving aside his shirt, Megan didn't give him any time. Her hands roamed his cold skin, heating it up. Impatient, he ripped the buttons off her blouse and threw it aside. Megan didn't even complain as she worked on the opening to his jeans.

This time when he entered her, along with incredible pleasure he felt a sense of coming home. Thank God he'd come after her.

Afterward, when Chad pulled her into his arms and held her against him, dropping occasional kisses on her lips, Megan waited for the words that would wound her. Now he would talk about visiting her. An occasional rendezvous. The pleasures they would share.

"You know, I'd planned to visit you in a couple of weeks," he said, as if they were sitting across from each other at the kitchen table at the ranch instead of naked, wrapped in each other's arms in her bed.

She stiffened in spite of her efforts to remain relaxed. After all, she'd expected those words.

"Meggie? What's wrong."

"Nothing. You were saying?"

"That was my solution to your leaving."

"Ah."

He kissed her neck and then her lips again. "But that won't work."

"What—what won't work?"

He rose up on one elbow and stared down at her, his brown eyes almost golden. "I love you, Meggie. I can't wait a couple of weeks."

Had she heard him right? She blinked rapidly, unsure whether to believe him. And still unsure where the conversation was going.

"Aren't you going to say anything?"

What else could she say? "I—I love you, too."

She was rewarded with an incredible kiss that consumed her. Her arms went around his neck, and she clung to him, pressing against him. She discovered he was ready for her again, too.

Later, when she was again in his arms, her heart a little less frightened, he chuckled sleepily. "We're going to have to be careful what we say, or I may die from exhaustion before I reach thirty."

There was some comfort in his words, since he had four years to go before he reached the advanced age of thirty. Four years to enjoy what had just occurred. And four years to worry about the end of it.

But all the tension, followed by the two incredible releases of it, had left her exhausted and she snuggled up against him. Like Scarlett, she'd worry about the future tomorrow. At least she could enjoy today.

HER BED WAS EMPTY when Megan awoke the next morning. Panic set in. He'd left her already? Had her happiness lasted only one night?

The sound of someone in her living room halted the ugly thoughts racing through her. She shoved back the covers and pulled on her robe.

She tiptoed to the door of the living room and discovered Chad sitting on the couch, writing. What was he writing, a letter? Was he writing her a goodbye note?

"Chad?"

"Morning, sleepyhead. Where's my morning kiss?" He grinned at her and held out his hand.

Only slightly reassured, she circled the couch and sat beside him, meeting his lips with hers. "What are you writing?" she then asked, holding her breath.

"Well, I've been up for a while, and I've been doing some thinking."

She tensed up, holding her breath. "You've got to go back to the ranch?"

His mouth covered hers, and his kiss was almost enough to make her forget what she thought he'd been trying to say. Almost.

"Woman, you're going to drive me crazy!" he muttered as soon as he got his breath back. "Haven't you figured out I can't survive without you?"

"What—what do you mean?"

"Why do you think I flew down here after you? For another night of good sex?" He kissed her again. "Hell, Megan, I want a lot more than that. You're coming back to the ranch with me."

She closed her eyes to gather strength. "I can't do that, Chad."

"Why not? Didn't you like living on the ranch?"

"Of course I did, but—but I can't just come live on the ranch. Jake wouldn't—"

"You think I'm asking you to live on the ranch as my lover?" Chad asked incredulously. "Sweetheart, you're out of your head."

She stared at him, irritated.

He didn't give her a chance to ask any questions. "You'll come as my wife. You'll come as Megan Chase Randall. And you'll never leave me."

His words were her dream, of course, but how could she believe him? He'd said he never intended to marry.

Some of her doubt must've shown in her eyes, because he leaned closer. "You don't believe me, do you?"

Not willing to admit he was right, she couldn't meet his gaze.

"I thought you might have a hard time believing me." The tenderness in his voice drew her to him.

"You did?"

"Yeah, and I don't want you to have any doubts. So I've drawn up a pre-nuptial agreement."

Stricken, she stared at him. Then she leapt from the sofa. "Get out!" she ordered, hoping to hold back the tears until he was gone.

The man was already planning for their divorce, just like her mother and each of her husbands. And he thought it would reassure her. She sobbed, almost hysterical at the irony of his actions.

"There you go, jumping to conclusions again," he said softly, not moving.

"The only conclusion I can see is that you're already planning for our marriage to fail. What do I get, a little money and my wedding band?" Her voice was vicious, but she didn't care.

"Nope," he replied, staring at her. "You should read it."

"I won't! I don't want any part of it. I don't want any part of you! I want you to leave!"

"That's not what you said last night."

She couldn't believe he was sitting there calmly on the couch. Opening her mouth to again insist he leave, she was stunned when he grabbed her hand and pulled her into his lap.

"What you get is my share of the Randall ranch."

"I don't care what— What did you say?"

He dropped a kiss on her lips and then laughed at her stunned expression. "Last night I got the feeling you still weren't sure about us, so I tried to think of some way to make you believe me. The most important thing in the world to me, after you, is the ranch. If I leave you, or betray you in any way, it's yours. We'll draw it up legally, and I'll sign on the dotted line."

"But, Chad—" she began, but she couldn't go on. He sat holding her against him, patiently waiting. "How can you do that?" she said finally. "How can you trust me with your most precious thing?"

"Because I've already trusted the most precious things to you, sweetheart. I've given you my heart . . . and my future. Without you, they all mean nothing." He kissed her again and then whispered,

"With you, I have everything. And I'm never planning to leave you."

"Me, neither," she whispered, her heart at peace at last.

"HOT DAMN!" Jake exclaimed, turning away from the phone to face his brothers.

"What is it?" Pete asked.

"It worked! My plan worked. Chad and Megan are getting married."

"That's good news," Brett said, a big smile on his face. "Guess we'll be having those babies, after all."

Red frowned. "I'm not changing no diapers. I did enough of that when Chad was a little 'un."

"It'll be awhile before we have to worry about that, Red," Jake assured him. Then he looked at his brothers. "But we need to work on a few more marriages around here."

"Hey, Jake," Pete protested, joined in by Brett. "You got lucky with Chad. Don't press your luck."

Jake eyed them, a grin on his face. "We'll just see about that."

We're thrilled to bring you another special edition of the popular MORE THAN MEN series.

Like those who have come before him, John Jarvis is more than tall, dark and handsome. All of those men have extraordinary powers that make them "more than men." But whether they are able to grant you three wishes, or live forever, make no mistake—their greatest, most extraordinary power is of seduction.

So make a date with John Jarvis in...

**#656 RED-HOT RANCHMAN
by Victoria Pade
November 1996**

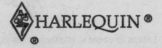